THE
BIBLE
IN RHYME

THE
BIBLE
IN RHYME

ANTHONY PISTILLI

iUniverse

THE BIBLE IN RHYME

iUniverse books may be ordered through booksellers or by contacting:

iUniverse
1663 Liberty Drive
Bloomington, IN 47403
www.iuniverse.com
844-349-9409

ISBN: 978-1-6632-2591-7 (sc)
ISBN: 978-1-6632-2592-4 (e)

Print information available on the last page.

iUniverse rev. date: 07/14/2021

THE OLD TESTAMENT

GENESIS

Till this moment, nothing, no creation, no light, no dark
There's only God, God is love, then His love's a fiery spark
'Let there be light!' Comes the Creator's sudden mighty call
Now comes water God parts it leaving land, sky, seas, and all
God makes man but woman too in His own image and guise
Dwell together they in the Garden of Eden, a gifted paradise

Takes place in 6 days the 7th, the Lord rests, in His good time
But there is so much more to tell in this our Biblical rhyme

NOAH

‿

Because in God's flawless work there's now found foul flaw
Eve, then Adam, Cain, all of them no longer hold God in awe
So God begins again. Wiping out mankind in order to save it
Judging the world. It's His divine judgment. And He gave it
God finds Noah. A man of faith. He tells Noah build an ark
But Noah's from the desert. Arks in his mind make no mark
God says an ark is like a boat. Noah asks, 'What's a boat?'
'Listen to me, Noah, an Ark is like a boat, an Ark will float.'
'Build the ark for all animals' God says, 'And for your folk.'
And so obeying God, Noah builds that ark, stroke by stroke
They've no truth no faith flood comes obedient to their doom
They try to clamor aboard Noah's Ark but there is no room

More than just family and animals are saved on Noah's Ark
All humanity! He calms the seas taking man out of the dark
But before God can yet give the world His complete embrace
He must first draw together a very most special blessed race
There will be a man named Abram, like Noah, his faith true
But that is a deep, eventful, golden story we've yet to come to
So, 'Come out of the Ark,' is now God's majestic command
And Noah's family and all the animals scatter onto dry land
Thus God chose faithful Noah to continue God's divine plan
But alas who is more dishonest and more wicked, than man?
Man will sin again and again doing all sins that can be done
God will save us once again. This time He gives His only Son

ABRAHAM

Now ages ago, in a city called Ur
So long ago that time itself does blur
The Bible tells us there's a couple named Sarai and Abram
Whose lives the Bible says we are to exhibit and are to exam
A descendant of Noah, 75, Abram's strong. Sarai is a beauty
Their sorrow is no children. Sarai can't do her marital duty
Now in the city of Ur there is this holy shrine
There the gods are many, pagan gods all set in line
There the goats are sacrificed from high altar to high altar
Where the priest cuts each goat's throat, he mustn't faulter
Abram is there this day attending this great prerogative rite
When a Voice speaks only to him, coming from a loving light
'Abram!' It is God's clear, full, free, bold, thunderous, Voice
Abram doesn't know it yet, he is God's most singular choice
'Leave country, people family. I'll send you to another land.'
This is God but how will he ever obey God's stern command
The priest to heathen gods makes further futile incantation
But all Abram hears: 'I will make you into a great nation.'
First it was Noah now Abram God has picked for this task
God knew Abram would say yes before God would even ask
Abram's nephew Lot and Lot's wife standing in the doorway
As Abram runs tell his wife, 'Sarai, God spoke to me today!'
'Which God?' 'Which God?' And he looks at her askance
'You think believing in just one God we're taking a chance?
'This is thee God. He's chosen me. What I'm saying is true.

3

We'll go to a land where we'll have children me and you.'
'Oh, Abram, I do so deeply want to give you a good son.
But leave home for some unknown land can that be done?'
'Sarai, you are my good wife.
And I love you more than life.
But God's made a promise, a covenant, promise He'll keep.
Faith will lead us to the land where we will laugh and leap.
Sarai, ready for the heirs of a new nation it will make us?'
Sarai takes Abram's hand. Her face full of tears. 'Take us.'

So they go, nephew Lot, Lot's wife, with a large household
Seeing by what great power Abram is made so sudden-bold
Sarai brings her slave woman, an Egyptian named Hagar
They go north, then west, trusting God, they go off very far
They travel through a desert city known as Haran
Then finally to a beautiful bountiful piece of land
But the land was not known to be very great in any size
And worse, Lot's wife shows herself to have jealous eyes
Fueled by Lot's mistrustful wife, a family feud grows too hot
One side following Abram. Other side following nephew Lot
The fate of the feud finally takes fire as all such feuds must
When two shepherds are found fighting in the dirt and dust
Lot and Lot's wife race to the cruel, vicious fight
Then Abram arrives taking in this dismal sight
'You're stealing our land.' Lot's wife's lips make a hot hiss
'God gave it to us to share.' Abram says. 'This land, this!'
'Lot, tell Abram there's not enough land, we've decided.'
'Have faith,' says Abram. 'This land the Lord's provided.'
Lot's wife laughs, 'Have faith in your God we cannot see?'
'We're leaving.' 'Leaving, Lot? What are you telling me?'
'We must leave.' 'Lot,' Abram asks. 'Where will you go?'
'Near Sodom.' 'Sodom! Vicious, evil Sodom! A city I know!'
Lot's wife says, 'In Sodom they give bliss a different treat
And when we go to Sodom we'll not starve, but we'll eat.'

On the hilltop Abram is standing, thinking, praying, alone
This is where he's built an altar to honor God, stone by stone
From this hill he can see all his people in the valley below
He sees Lot heading for Sodom praying as he sees him go
Thanking God for the Promised Land. 'It's all that I adore.'
God speaks, 'It's all to you and your offspring forevermore.'
On the altar Abram offers his sacrifice, he is so very grateful
He's worried by Lot's leaving. And Lot's wife, she is hateful
He continues to miss Lot. At the altar he continues to pray
Then one day he is surprised to see a man limping his way
It's Lemuel, Lot's shepherd. 'How could this be our plight?
We were beaten by henchmen. It was a wicked Sodom fight.
Lot's their prisoner. It's a terrible thrashing they gave us.'
He says to Abram. 'You're the only one who can save us.'

Abram gathers all the families. They all talk into the night
'We have brave men among us,' Abram says. 'We'll fight!'
Serai protests. 'Lot left on his own. Abram, this is madness!'
Leaving for Sodom Abram's shepherds leave behind sadness
Abram's shepherds now to the hills outside Sodom they'll go
Where carefully, cautiously, they'll steal right up to their foe
Lot and his wife are imprisoned by soldiers in their guard
The soldiers revel, tipple, and treat them ever ever so hard
Abram looks at his men, about 300, all willing but untried
The enemy is in the thousands, an attack would be suicide
But God has given him two things with grace and favor
One is ambush below, the other is faith, faith's the saver
'Trust in God!', and Abram orders his shepherds to attack
Taken by surprise, beaten, the enemy is thrown on its back
Abram finds Lot. 'This is God's triumph.' Lot looks away
'Lot, do you have something bad to say on this great day?'
'We're going back to Sodom. There where things are better.'
'Think of those who died for you here! You're their debtor.'
'I know I am. I can never repay what I owe.
But still to Sodom, my wife and I must go.'

5

'Lot you must keep faith. How many times must I repeat it?'
'Drink faith?' Lot's wife asks. 'Clothe us? Can we eat it?'
'More, God's promised nation for you, for Serai, everyone.'
'And how when your own wife will never bear you a son?'
'No,' she says. "We care about food, water and shelter.'
Wracked with emotional pain, Abram wants to belt her
'Lot, you must come back to all those people that you know.'
'No, Uncle, today, my wife and I to Sodom we both must go.'

So Abram returns to the Promised Land to bury the dead
He must see Serai to say she was right in all that she said
It was she who said Lot and his wife had chosen to be lost
She had trusted Abram, he let her down, all at such a cost

Abram's the ancestor of offspring as countless as the stars
He trusts in all that God pledged, and his faith will be ours
But just when will that son to his good wife Serai be born?
That he will be the father of many nations seems so forlorn
Sarai tells Abram, 'I tried to move God by my fair prayer.
But now I must tell you, I cannot have children. I am bare.
But it is only God's plan and purpose that we must fulfill.'
'What?' Asks Abram. Sarai says, 'We'll still do God's will.
You shall take my Egyptian servant Hagar. Go to her tent.'
'No,' says Abram. 'Yes,' says Sarai, 'Go with my consent.
The stars God's promised need at least one heir.
And this may be how God is answering our prayer.
So Abram leaves for Hagar's tent
As he leaves Sarai's heart is rent

What did they do, Abram and Sarai?
That fateful night? That fateful day?
Abram thinks, 'What's done is done.'
On their own they gave themselves a son

Whatever they deserve, however you see their endeavor
Abram's visit in Hagar's tent will change the world forever

Ishmael, Abram's son by Hagar is now thirteen years old
A joy to Abram. Ishmael is kind, caring, vigorous, and bold

Abram is 99, Sarai is 90, they live in an oasis for many years
When Serai sees Ishmael she questions herself by her fears
'God could have made me with child, what have I created?
God provides all things. Dear God, I should have waited!'
One day when Abram is sitting in the shade on the ground
The Lord appears to Abram and Abram falls facedown
He is now Abraham, Serai is Sarah and males give foreskin
This is circumcision a hope that it will lead to no more sin
And then God says, 'To a son Sarah is to give birth.'
Abraham laughs. God avers. Why not? God created earth?
Not long after three men walk towards Abraham's tent
What Abraham doesn't know yet is that they're heaven sent
Thank the good Lord that Abraham acted wise
For two of them are angels, but the third is God in disguise
With Abraham, the Lord again made that prediction so bold
'I promise a son.' Outside, Sarah laughs, 'We're too old.'
'You laughed.' 'No.' 'When your son comes I'll come after.
So you won't forget name him Isaac which means laughter.'
Abraham sees it's God to whom he's been trying to be a host
God says He will destroy Sodom which means Lot the most
Stunned yet he finds the courage deep within to concentrate
With God, the God he loves, Abraham, is about to negotiate
As proof of His promise God agrees Sodom he will spare
If there are just 50 righteous people found there
Then He agrees to 45, then 40, then 30, and then just 10
It'll only be Lot who must save his family for that time when

Here at Sodom where there is so much sex-making
Sex of all kinds. He-sex and she-sex, bought-sex, sex-taking
Lot sees these people far from God as he sits at the city gate
He wants to leave. His wife won't go. The evening grows late
Two men come up. There's something in them he can feel
'Come to my home where I can offer you a bed and a meal.'
These are two angels of God and then what happens next
Sodomites surround Lot's house. They want to have sex!
One angel stands up making some kind of gesture or sign
As the angel does this the mob outside go suddenly blind
The angels reveal themselves as warriors sent by the Lord
One plunges himself into the mob slashing with his sword
The other tells Lot's family, 'To go,' he says in a calm voice
In the presence of the angel they know they have no choice
'You and all your family must get out before it's too late!
Sodom is done get out quickly or you'll suffer the same fate!'
The angels protect Lot's family as Sodom explodes in flame
Praying on a hillside Abraham sees Sodom suffer its blame
Sodom is wrapped in fire. Roofs collapsing. Falling beams
Pain! Suffering! Such an agony is only ended by screams
The angels say, 'Run, never look back. No matter what!'
They disappear. His family's safe. All before an amazed Lot
They run, not away, but to what they hope will be a new life
There is one last burst of light. Who looks back? Lots wife
And because of this woman's fault
Lot's wife turns into a pillar of salt

Time passes, noiselessly, step by step it steals away
We're with Sarah where God's prophecy comes true today
Abraham is outside while inside Sarah is howling wild
These screams to Abraham are music they mean a child
Abraham steps in. Sarah, holding a child, whispers, 'A boy.'
'Just as God promised. We shall name him Isaac. Such joy.'

Time has leaped a year, but in camp there is great tension
Sarah and Hagar have much bitter and envious dissension
They struggle between them for Abraham's attention
And then ask which son will get his rightful ascension
The Lord says it's Isaac to whom the inheritance must go
Hagar, Ishmael must leave. Abraham thinks this a bad blow
God says, 'I've made both you and Isaac one foundation.
Ishmael's children I will also make them a great nation.'
Alone in the desert Hagar prays with faith God gave them
God's Angel comes with a well filled with water to save them

Isaac is 10. Sarah's a good mother, giving her love carefully
Abraham feels he's not the leader God intended him to be
God speaks again this time wanting Isaac as a blood sacrifice
Isaac God wants back? Who can afford to pay such a price?
On an altar into Isaac's heart he's ready to plunge the knife
Angel calls, 'Now I know you fear God, do not take his life.
Since for Me you were prepared to let your only son die.
God gives you descendants as numerous as stars in the sky.'
Rejoicing Abraham's kissing Isaac Isaac's kissing Abraham
The angel's gone. They see God's delivered a sacrificial lamb
Sarah finds them, 'Praise God! Praise God! We are Blessed!'
Yes his faith in God has been put to trial and it stood the test

JOSEPH

Abraham dies but 12 tribes from his grandsons will be found
Jacob has Joseph, with that father's love Joseph's crowned
As token of Jacob's love Joseph receives a multicolored robe
Bad brothers want him gone. Any way they can they'll probe
Beat and kick him! How could brothers make such knavery?
Worse! For a bag of coins they sell him into Egyptian slavery
They dip the robe in goat's blood say he's killed by a beast
Jacob buries his face in the robe crying, 'Joseph's deceased!'
Sold to a rich Egyptian family, he's assured a life of ease
The owner's wife wants to bed him, but he refuses to please
Rejected by Joseph there is no way then to stop her
She says that it was Joseph, not she, who is being improper
He's thrown into prison. It's filthy, foul prison that he is cast
He is so dirty since in this vile prison so much time has past
A baker and a cupbearer are imprisoned there too
He interprets two dreams for both that turn out to be true
Then he's taken to the Pharaoh the cupbearer is at his side
'No one can explain my dream, but you can if you tried.'
The Pharaoh recounts the fierce vexation of his dream
'Pharaoh there's only one view of this dream, one theme.
There'll be famine. You must store food for that day.
Store grain or you'll watch your Kingdom slip away.'
Pharaoh says, 'I am impressed by all that you have revealed.
Your free but you make them store grain from their yield.'

The famine is foiled and now Joseph will run things
Next to the mighty Pharaoh it's as if there were two kings
It reaches other places, other people are suffering great pain
Because of Joseph these people come to Egypt for their grain
Among these people were none other than Joseph's brothers
Should he make them slaves? Or treat them like the others?
He tricks them into thinking he's a difficult ruling entity
Brings their father to Egypt, then reveals his true identity

1000's of Israel slaves are now doing what Pharaoh imposes
But they will be saved by a killer, a castaway. He is Moses

MOSES

Abraham's children are as stars. God's promised prediction
The Pharaoh kills boys at birth that's their further affliction
One's saved. Moses. Cast onto the Nile, but onto still water
God guides that basket into the hands Pharaoh's daughter
Raised a prince, in sight, all thought this tale to be true
Few know, least of all Prince Moses, that he is a Hebrew
With Rameses, Pharaoh's son, Moses scar's him in a duel
Learns he's a Hebrew he kills a slave master for being cruel

40 years pass. Moses is in Arabia, from Egypt he is quite far
Rameses is the new Pharaoh, and has not forgotten that scar
One day God speaks. The burning bush. God's love burning!
And suddenly from the bottom of Moses' soul he is learning!
Then God tells Moses what he must now show himself to be
'Yes Lord, I will return to Egypt. I will set my people, free.'
He finds his people still enslaved. Their faith dull and barren
He finds a good man Joshua. Sister Miriam. Brother Aaron
God sends 10 plagues to Egypt before the Pharaoh will agree
To make them truly 'Free at last'. He even parts the Red Sea
Now they'll follow Moses wherever God tells Moses to go
40 years waiting for that Promised Land for God to show
God also gives them commandments in stone. There are ten
A plan for man to live by, to seek spirituality time and again
His 120th birthday God buries Moses in an unknown grave
Joshua finds them the Promise land based on all Moses gave

JOSHUA

40 years since Pharaoh and to the Promised Land they go
60 year old Joshua leads them to the walls outside Jericho
Into the city for reconnaissance he has sent a pair of spies
People inside fear a siege once the Hebrews stop all supplies
A lone woman inside Jericho who by her beauty she will stab
Selling her body to make money the beauty's name is Rahab
The two spies move through Jericho with caution and dread
If they are caught first torture then each will lose their head
They try to hide, place to place, but who should they meet?
Soldiers! Canaanite Soldiers searching on a Jericho street
The rams horn is sounded the spies run, run, and hideaway
And God chose Rahab's house for them to hide in that day
Instead of turning over to soldiers both men does she hide
She's left a red cord, so the Hebrews know she is their guide
Spies return to say Jericho walls solid. Their hearts are not
Joshua knows they are too solid. He needs a plan and a plot
Joshua sits by the fire tries to think the whole thing through
A friend whirs into his mind, 'Moses, what would you do?'
One thing he knows Moses did, one thing he did every day
Moses would go somewhere, some mountain top and pray
So does Joshua. Alone he climbs a mountain. Lost in prayer
When out of nowhere the Lord's mighty warrior will appear
'March round the city for 6 days and on the 7th day shout
God will make all the walls of Jericho collapse and fall out.'

13

And when the walls fall it's an earthquake that will rumble
Rahab's red cord saves her then Jericho in dust it'll crumble
So that's how the Israelites take Jericho hacked by sword
Without walls to protect it Joshua gives Jericho to the Lord

50 years more with God's power Joshua's Hebrews he leads
Then he dies and they turn to other Gods to meet their needs
Oh mighty God is betrayed by all this and is much grieved
Sends the Hebrews 100's of years of punishment unrelieved
Of the foreign enemies in this time the Hebrews will've seen
None was more powerful or more deadly than the Philistine
They have conquered the Hebrews their land and their space
But God again returns the Hebrews to their Promised Place
And again to do this he chooses an unlikely spiritual scion
An eight year old named Samson. He's as strong as a lion!

SAMSON

It's been 150 years now since Joshua has been forever gone
Philistines now have control as the Israelites are withdrawn
There's been a barren woman praying. Her soul seems good
Today a Lord's angel appears his face half hidden by a hood
'Don't be afraid. You're to have a son. It is a gift from God.
But there are things you must do and follow, however hard.
Till the boy is born drink no alcohol and eat nothing unclean
His hair is not to be cut.' The angel then in a wink is unseen
The woman did all she is told. The boy is born. It is all done
Now thick head of head hair grows on young strong Samson
But Samson's done nothing to give the Israelites a better life
Drifting from God he's even ready to marry a Philistine wife
To the wedding Samson is lost, finds himself in a lion's den
A young lion leaps at Samson and it's in that moment when
He has God's strength to tear the lion apart with bare hands
There's bees buzzing the lion's carcass from where he stands
The buzzing gives a strange idea. This attack will not be told
He will keep it a secret. The lion. Bees. All will he withhold

At the wedding tween Philistines and Israelites much strain
Samson does feats of strength giving Philistines more pain
Warrior Abimilech is there. All of Israel he wants to muzzle
Samson will humble him by asking him an impossible puzzle
'I'll tell you a riddle, you must answer it within seven days
If not 30 linen garments, 30 sets of clothes the loser pays.'

15

These were terms Samson and Abimilech promised to meet
Out of eater something to eat out of strong something sweet
'What is sweeter than honey? What is stronger a lion?'
Abimilech seemed to find the answer without really trying
What he did was to threaten the bride's household to death
She gave in, now vengeance afflicts Samson's every breath

At the Philistine harvest all their wheat he will let burn
Abimilech then kills Samson's wife and family in return
Abimilech killing Samson's wife is an act of such deformity
Samson wages war on the Philistines with greater enormity
He is bursting with rage as he bursts into the Philistine fort
Killing countless soldiers throws them down onto the court
Releasing the Israelite prisoners he has opened every cell
Only beginning to get his revenge there's still more to tell

Abimilech kills two Hebrews a day. This wrong he renders
Samson, heeding his mother, but against his will, surrenders

Samson is now chained to a stone wall in the market square
Bleating of lambs and goats destined for slaughter fill the air
Abimilech comes up to him they stare into each other's eyes
Through gritted teeth, Samson says, 'You have your prize.'
'And we all thought your God made this Samson so strong.
I kill you, I'll send all you Israelites back where you belong.'
Israelites: 'They wanted Samson. That's who we gave them.'
They've sentenced to death he who could have saved them
The Philistine soldiers the Israelites there they begin to slay
Samson hears a voice. 'Lord?' It is You. What am I to say?
On the ground there's a donkey jawbone dirty and neglected
The Lord has this jawbone by Samson's gaze to be detected
God's voice gives him new power coursing through his veins
With a seeming simple shrug he breaks, shakes off his chains

Killing the soldiers with the dangling chains from his wrist
Shackling and hackling them, then their throats he'll twist
Then he grabs the jawbone wielding like a sword and an axe
Killing soldier after, after soldier, after soldier, who attacks
Finally all the Philistines they run and are now all scattered
'In my heart,' rages Samson. 'I have done all that mattered.'

Now he's alone in an alley and breathlessly falls on his knees
'Lord,' he asks, 'Is this what you want? Guide me, please.'
Suddenly a woman appears carrying water in a flask
To describe this woman's beauty is simply too great a task
Pouring him some water to drink she takes a little sip first
Forgetting all his wild rage Samson realizes his great thirst
'Who are you? And thanks for the water. I was ever so dry.'
'Delilah. I am Delilah.' And she is not only beautiful but shy

Samson and Delilah are now living together as man and wife
Abimilech sees this, hates it, he wants to take Samson's life
After offering Delilah thousands of pieces of silver in a chest
She will find from where his great strength is so possessed

So in that moment of closeness that every couple might share
He said it's his hair, over grown and never cut, his very hair

Content, happy Samson falls into a deep untroubled sleep
Delilah cuts his hair getting all that silver she wants to keep
Abimilech rushes in with his soldiers. Samson's weak, afraid
Silver is thrown over his hair on the bed. He's been betrayed
He sees Delilah. How could she? So loving, so giving, so kind
Abimilech puts thumbs in Samson's eyes. Samson is blind

Samson is in chains again. Both eyes have been plunged in
For months now he's been kept in a deep loathsome dungeon
Tortured, tormented by soldiers, they beat him every day
Pummel him with fists and clubs his body raw they flay
Dragged to a Pagan temple where by Philistines he's taunted
He knows Delilah must be there, by her image he is haunted
As they yell and spit they put him up against the central post
'God,' Samson says, 'Your power now. I need it the most.'
Leaning hard on the pillar within him his strength grew
Running up Abimilech asks, 'What are you trying to do?'
A cloud of dust comes down as the temple begins to shake
Fear fills the room, people stare at Samson as pillars quake
'This can't be!' cries Abimilech. 'Your locks were shorn!
From you your power should have been ripped and torn!'
'Those locks were just a visual reminder of God's accord.
Power always comes from God of the Israelites, our Lord.'
Finally Samson stops pushing. The pillars have been parted
The temple is collapsing. He has finished what he started
'Lord I'll die with the Philistines.' He's proud to be humble
God grants Samson's prayer. The entire temple will crumble

Samson's triumph is brief, much, much too brief
The Philistines continue to wage war and bring grief
In the midst of this mayhem God sends a man who is pure
That man's Prophet Samuel you've heard of him I'm sure
Not only will it be the evil Philistines that he disposes
But he'll be the greatest spiritual mentor since Moses

SAMUEL

Again God has not spoken to his people in many many years
Again a barren woman is given a son named 'God He Hears'
This is the prophet Samuel who unveils God's great mystery
Through him God is going to change Israel's eventful history

It was the Philistines. And again Israelites to be defeated
When Samuel sacrificed to Lord for victory he entreated
The Lord sent a great flood making the Philistines sinkable
A great wind across their army making advance unthinkable
Philistines retreated and ran as fast as their feet could trod
And the Israelites thank Samuel for this. Samuel and God

Later he learns two sons are corrupt. 'They take presents!'
Now the Israelite people will be "crowned" by these events
'Just tell me,' Samuel says. 'And I'll help you in everything.'
Words that will change the Israelite people forever: 'A king.'

Alone on top of a hill he speaks golden words with the Lord
A King Lord? But king will be fickle, false and full of fraud
'I'll give them a man who can lead them, lead them, all in all
A keen swordman who gives fearful battle. His name is Saul.
'But,' says the Lord, 'There is much more I am going to do.
You, Samuel, as My Prophet are going to lead them, too.'

But they could not rule together all they had were fights
Saul turns away from Samuel giving all a grief that smites
So Samuel the Prophet is now out searching for a new king
You and I know that it will be David the Israelite true king

DAVID

❧

Samuel leaves Saul to find and anoint David he must go
David's direct descendent is Jesus of Nazareth we all know
Saul and his son Jonathan keep winning, continue to win
Battle after battle, but Saul's heart is filled with chagrin
He finds no peace in victory. He's worn down by being king
From his last fight with Samuel he still feels the sharp sting
He continues to ask that when Samuel left on that one day
Did Samuel the prophet take not only himself but God away
Even in his sleep these fears haunt him in his ghastly dreams
'Lord, please, I beg you, forgive me, forgive,!' He screams

Saul's young armor bearer brings him a filled cup of water
Saul is still planning how to lure the Philistines to slaughter
Saul pays no heed to the lad helping him put on his armor
No more than a disdainful shepherd, perhaps a poor farmer
Suddenly Jonathan breathlessly rushes into Saul's tent
'Father, come immediately!' What could be so urgent?
They rush to see before their army standing
A very bad 9 foot tall, tall giant demanding
To fight one Israelite just one, just him, just one
If Israelite wins we Philistines will be their slaves, done
But if he wins Israelites will be Philistines slaves, agree?
'Surely there is one courageous enough to fight just me.
Just one soldier come forward.' Goliath continues his rant
The fear of death seizes each Israelite soldier, and they can't

'Your God is weaker than our gods' They beat their shields
The Israelite Army in silence in shame, in bitterness it yields
'I thought you people followed this God of yours, this Lord.'
'Someone must fight him,' and Jonathan finds his sword
'No,' says Saul calmly, 'This is a trap, put your sword away.
No one's going to fight this giant this huge hill of flesh today'
'I'll do it!' A boy's calm sure voice answers Goliath's call
It's David, the lowly shepherd, the armor bearer for Saul
Saul to David, 'You are no soldier all you know are sheep.'
'I kept them safe,' David says, 'Now God it's me He'll keep.
I can fight this uncircumcised Philistine, him I can destroy.'
Saul replies, 'You're just an armor bearer, a shepherd boy.'
'For years I've been protecting sheep on my father's lands
And now our God has placed your protection in my hands'
David heads to battle with the giant just a sling and a stone
He stands before the giant. Saying nothing. Just David alone
'Don't waste my time little boy, you are too young to die.'
'You've the sword and spear but it is our Lord you defy.'
Goliath rushes on David as he spins the sling round his head
The stone lets fly. It hits the giant. He falls to ground. Dead
With the giant's sword he severs his head and holds it high
Signal for Israeli Army to slay the Philistines as they race by

Saul to David, 'You are such a wise boy, good and discreet.
Here's a sword more befitting. We have an enemy to defeat.'

Years pass, David defeats Israel's enemies, defeats them all
Fighting alongside his good friend Jonathan, and King Saul
Israelite's believe there is nothing David cannot overcome
A noble hero, a great leader is what David now has become
What he never shares when Samuel had the power to choose
Is Samuel and God anointed him to become King of the Jews
The prophet's words in his ears he can still hear them ring
The words of Samuel saying someday he will be Israel's king

Saul killed thousands! The crowd cheers and cheers
David killed tens of thousands! Someone volunteers
Saul's smile vanishes. It's replaced by a dark angry frown
He looks at David. 'Next they'll say he deserves my crown.'
Filled with murderous envy it's David he wants to slaughter
He offers David the hand in marriage of Michal his daughter
David must slay 100 Philistines bring Saul their foreskins
Again here is King Saul committing more and more sins
An impossible task, yet one for which David will fully strive
Saul's plan is simple. David will die. He will not return alive
But of course to Saul's and to everyone's complete surprise
David does return with 200 of what he'd taken for that prize
He marries Michal. But now this tale will be filled with woe
For he and King Saul will now be one another's bitter foe
Saul believes he and David are fighting to be Israel's king
So against David now Saul will use everything and anything

David must run away. There are those who to him are kind
Saul gives chase leaving a wake of violence, mayhem behind
At a shrine it was learned priests sheltered David for a night
He cut priests throats right then and there in broad daylight

Saul finds himself praying alone in a cool mountainous cave
Unknown is a hooded man behind a rock it's David so brave
'I could have just killed you, but I will not kill you ever.'
'You promise to not wipe out my name.' David: 'Never.'
So to Saul's prayer this is a message that the Lord did bring
It is all just a matter of time this is the man who will be king

'Father' Jonathan cries. 'The Philistine army is near.'
'The Philistine Army? It is David that I need to fear.'
'Forget David! There is your kingdom you must defend!'
'We leave at dawn. There is something that I must attend.'

He walks into the night dazed, with a tedious taste of tedium
He steps into the light of a fire into the presence of a medium
Medium is an old woman in a trance about to be addressed
'Bring up the dead prophet Samuel.' Saul's simple request
Samuel appears next to Saul sitting on a rock
Saul is now in complete and utter shock
'Why did you wake me? Why disturb my spirit?'
'I called you when I speak to the Lord He does not hear it.'
'You disobeyed. That's why there's silence when you pray.'
'I tried, I tried to obey the Lord. The Lord, I tried to obey.'
'This battle is your last, you'll be with me as will your son.'
'Take me! Take me!' Saul begs. 'But spare Jonathan!'
Now all that Saul hears is wind. The ghost of Samuel is gone
He must face the day and death he must put battle armor on
Jonathan shot by an arrow, Samuel's prophecy comes true
Saul falling on his sword dies sorrowfully and slowly, too

While this is the end of Saul it is David's beginning
In time all of Israel's tribes David will be winning
Next he will need a city from which to reign and rule
That city is a crossroads, with fresh water, a jewel
Calls it Jerusalem, Ark of the Covenant a proper place
While celebrating his victory he sees a beautiful face
Her name's Bathsheba, she's Uriah, his captain's wife
He thinks he's never seen anyone so ravishing in his life
Man is sin. David no longer follows the Lord's good path
From his roof everyday he watches Bathsheba take a bath
The House of David rule Israel forever says prophet Nathan
'A son builds God's temple all the people will have faith in.'
A stunned David turns away from Bathsheba he is distracted
But soon turns to the vision below. To her he is so attracted
Forcing himself not to think about God, no consultary
He covets his neighbor's wife and commits adultery

And because King David's bed they had defiled
At that time he got Uriah's wife, Bathsheba, with child
He tries to have Uriah be the father. That plan falls through
Then he has Uriah killed in battle. Such sins a man dare do

He makes Bathsheba Queen, she bears a son, all in good time
David God's King of Israel, has committed the perfect crime
But God knows. Sends His prophet Nathan to see the king
That God looked on David and saw everything. Everything!
'The Lord has spoken to me, our Lord, God and our Master.
And this I say. That on your house he'll soon bring disaster.'
By these sharp words he's stung. 'But I am His chosen one!'
'You'll not die, there'll be a result from what you've done.'
'I have sinned! I have sinned!' And David's son begins to cry
Result of all David's sinning. It is David's son who has to die
Nathan tells David he didn't rule in God's name but his own
But God still truly loves him and will let him keep his throne
And says to Bathsheba, 'And he will grant you another son.'
And the name of that son, that well-known name, is Solomon
In Jerusalem he builds the temple just as Nathan predicted
It is where the Ark of the Covenant will be forever depicted
Solomon is all wise his time is one of prosperity and of peace
There comes a time for him when following God shall cease

After Solomon dies power goes on to corrupt Israel's kings
Keeping God's kingdom on earth the most of hardest things
Dreadful bloody civil war will split the nation right in two
Prophets say turn to God. They don't. When do they ever do
Northern Kingdom by the Assyrian Army will be destroyed
Southern Kingdom by slavery it'll be carried and made void
New prophet Daniel speaks of dream telling of a new king
Daniel doesn't know. This is Jesus who'll change everything

DANIEL

The years have passed for Israel. They have gone on and on
They are now all ruled by King Nebuchadnezzar of Babylon
So this pagan King to Babylon all the Israelites he has taken
And the Israelites their God of Abraham they have forsaken
There is one-Daniel-blessed in a strange way during the exile
He interprets dreams and the food at court he does not defile
And so the King had a dream no one knew what it meant
And that is when it was Daniel for whom the King sent
The King dreamed of a golden statue. 'Follow this path?'
Daniel said to build such a statue would invite God's wrath
The King is intrigued by this God, but he acts more boldly
He builds the statue anyway, making it even more goldly
Three friends of Daniel refuse to worship and adore it
Ordered to be burned men take oil on them and pore it
Set afire from the flames they were smothered and smoked
There's 4th person with them. It's the Holy Spirit uncloaked
God showed up. The 3 men are fine. The King's impressed
Captive Jews now worship their God in peace and have rest

Time passes and the great King of Babylon has gone insane
It is only Daniel who copes with the King in courteous pain
Then this King of Babylon is conquered by a Persian King
And our Daniel loses not only influence, he loses everything
He appeals to the conquering King set his people free when
King throws him in a dungeon. There's a roar. A lion's den

Daniel falls on the floor full of fear. His eyes so full of tears
He prays and prays to the Lord suddenly an angel appears
The angel says to Daniel that you are innocent in God's eyes
For Daniel, all fear's gone. Rises to his feet. Every tear dries
All the lions and now Daniel they simply lie down and rest
Then the Persian King sees Daniel sleeping on a lion's chest
The Persian decrees Jews return to Jerusalem. Exile done
He returns their looted treasures rebuilding has now begun
40 thousand Israelites march back to their Promised Land
Daniel stayed. His home's here. This is what God planned
He has more bold Israelite visions. Nations will enslave them
Turning away from God again, and all that God gave them
Daniel has also another bold vision. It is of the Son of Man
Descended from David. King of Jews. It is God's great plan

THE NEW TESTAMENT

500 years will see but more subservience in time's fair course
First Macedon, then Rome takes Israel by fire and by force
The Israelites are now ruled by that Roman puppet Herod
Before him, their faith and fortune stands naked and arid
But the more they are beaten down they keep looking higher
They're waiting in hopes of rescue by the promised Messiah

And the Messiah comes at first quietly giving very little note
It all takes place in Nazareth, just a village small and remote
That's where Joseph the carpenter is sitting behind a screen
He looks at Mary she's the most beautiful girl he's ever seen
Joseph's not a man of great vision. A carpenter. A good Jew
His faith will be needed to understand what is about to ensue

The breath of wind shovels in dust through street after street
The clatter of metal, swords, shields, sound of marching feet
Under the hot Judean sun Roman soldiers move in a lane
Come to collect tribute. Cloth. Leather. Fresh fruit. Grain
Mary walks home through this on a day like any other day
An angel of the Lord stands before her and he's going to say
'I am Gabriel, Lord has looked down upon you and smiled.
You have favor with God. Soon you will give birth to a child,
You're to call him Jesus. He'll be great and I'll tell thee why
For he will be known unto all as the Son of the Most High.'

'But I am still virgin.' 'The Holy Spirit will take over you.
Power of the Most High there'll be a great make over you.'
'I, Mary, am the Lord's servant. May it be to me as you say.
Jesus, I am to name him Jesus. I will never forget this day.'

To Joseph now her pregnancy she is going to have to explain
She knows that when he finds out he will feel such cruel pain
Cousin she hides the one who John the Baptist will give birth
But when she returns it is obvious Joseph notices her girth
'This is God's work. There has been no one. I swear to you.
An angel of the Lord appeared to me. I tell you what's true.'
Joseph turns away. He circles the room like animal in a cage
'Please I'm telling you the truth. You mustn't feel such rage'
'Yes, but why would He send the Messiah to us? Why?'
He walks out and doesn't look back. Then lets himself cry
Joseph wanders the streets so angry, worried, so frustrated
Then the Angel Gabriel appears to him, too, and he is elated
'Joseph, take Mary as your wife she speaks true she is pure.'
He's to protect Mary and this baby Jesus. Of that he's sure
They think Jesus is a Messiah save Israel from Roman sway
He will not just save Israel but the world on that fateful day
However much it may seem much too worse than senseless
Periodically it is the ruling Romans way to demand a census
Married, off to Bethlehem where King David was born
On their way there a brilliant star does their path adorn

Mary and Joseph are not alone in admiring that star
In faraway Babylon, a sage astrologer name Balthazar
He's now riding towards Israel following the heavenly clues
He's bound for Jerusalem eager to deliver the Good News
But he's taking it to the one man who doesn't want to hear it
King Herod. Rumors about a King of Jews and he will fear it

Joseph shows Mary, holds the newborn baby up to the light
A crowd starts to gather. That star has led many to this site
Ordinary people drawn on this cold night to this small cave
These are the ones whom Jesus, the Son of God, came to save
Balthazar meets Nubian wise men on their way to Bethlehem
They don't truly know who Jesus is or what's awaiting them
Balthazar, the fine kings, they all brings gifts, and bow down
They ask the name of child, 'Jesus'. Then fall on the ground

And so the crowd departs and drifts off well into the night
The Magi do not return to tell Herod of this wondrous sight
Because they had all learned quickly in a vision and a dream
That for the infant Jesus Herod has a cruel-hearted scheme
Joseph too has a vision and dream where all he sees is blood
Makes him know what he must do. It comes to him in a flood
Herod soldiers killed every male child dragged them scraped
But the one child Herod wants, Jesus, He's already escaped

They make a home for themselves in Egypt and they wait
In 5 years they return. Herod is dead. Rome runs the state
When Jesus is 12 Joseph decides to further his education
It's off to Jerusalem just in time for a ritual and celebration
This is why His family goes to Jerusalem. Why they migrate
1000's of like-minded pilgrims come every year to celebrate

Joseph, Mary are swept away by Passover it is so delightful
But when the holiday is over Jesus is missing this is frightful
After searching all parts of the ancient city they are reaching
They are led inside the Temple where they see Jesus teaching
'What does God say about Justice?' asked a priest who's old
Jesus said, It's written in Isaiah, where the answer is told.
They will be a safe place from stormy winds and a rock.
Mary, Joseph break through the circle. They freeze in shock

31

'Jesus', says Mary. 'We've been looking all this while.'
I had to be in my father's house. He says with a smile

Jesus returns to Nazareth there He will see Joseph's passing
20 years, physically, emotionally, spiritually, He is amassing

Jesus must reach the entire world His voice is unique
But first comes John the Baptist the man the Jews seek
This man from the wilderness he heard the Holy Spirit's call
Now he baptizes in the River Jordon, young, old, baptizes all
Many that he baptizes believe that he John is the Messiah
'There is one to come more powerful than me, more higher.'
But then came Jesus. John sees Him. It all sudden and a stun
His entire life he's been waiting. This Jesus, he is the one
'You come to me to be baptized when I need baptism by you'
Let this be so for now, John. It is just proper for us to do.
With people looking on into the Jordon River Jesus is eased
God says: 'This is my beloved Son whom I am well pleased.'

Now comes desert where He fasts for 40 nights and 40 days
For that He meditates on the will of God He prays and prays
He knows what He's called upon to do, destiny is with Him
But He is against mighty Rome, He can be gone on a whim
Before He can reach all those souls that He can straighten
There's one spiritual leader that He must confront: Satan
Jesus is starved consumed by hunger for food He is craving
Before Him powerful serpent slithers past its tongue waving
'If You are the Son of God tell the stones to become bread'
Man shall not live bread alone but God's word Jesus said
Serpent turns and turns making thousands of grains of dust
Then this strange Serpent, who is Satan, vanishes in disgust
Jesus is dreaming. He's standing on top of the Temple roof
Satan is there to see if Jesus can find in His own heart proof

'If You are truly the Son of God then throw Yourself down
'Angels will come to save You before you hit the ground.'
Jesus says to Satan here is known well, it needn't be guessed
Jesus warns Satan: Don't put the Lord our God to the test.
Jesus now stands atop a cliff the view stretches to infinity
'I give you the world,' says Satan, 'if you will worship me.'
Get away, Satan! Worship our Lord and serve Him alone.
With Satan Jesus wrestled, the serpent was well overthrown
In the power of the Holy Spirit that is His strong condition
Walks out of the desert ready and sure to begin His mission

In Nazareth He says He's the Messiah their faith is tested
John the Baptist scolds young Herod so he is arrested
Herod violated God's law he married his brother's wife
John spoke the truth scolded Herod now it cost him his life

Now we've Peter, James, and John, trying to fill their nets
Fishermen from Galilee, nets empty, but they've no regrets
As they guide their boats to shore they see a figure waiting
They try not to notice but it's hard not to, He's captivating
'Who's that?' 'The Messiah, Peter.' 'Oh? Can He find fish?'
Jesus pulls Peter's boat into the water. I can if you wish.
What follows is a day of fishing unlike any other anywhere
Boats come. So many fish are caught that nets begin to tear
'Teacher,' says Peter, I'm just a fisherman, so full of sin.'
So follow me, Peter, you'll be a fisher of men, we'll begin.

Crowded market. Activity there simply never seems to cease
Comes a woman there tormented by a devil she has no peace
A running wildcat round the market yelling and screamin'
Possessed by some unmatchable low vile shameless demon
Running every which way until before Jesus she stands
Come out of her! Of the demons then Jesus commands

Demons' violent energy pours out of her as her face freezes
She's changed by His Spirit that He gives to who He pleases
What's your name? Asks Jesus. 'Mary Magdalene' Come.
Love one another. Know who I am and where I came from.

Word of Jesus' miracles spread these are His healing powers
Where ever He is hundreds go, the day has not enough hours
It grows with every footstep, mile, every village and town
People long to see Him or try to touch the hem of His gown

As all the disciples see for Jesus all this growing adulation
They ask could so much need have fallen upon Israel nation?

Then there is the cripple who sons lower him down the roof
Jesus heals him. All are dazzled. This is power of God. Proof
But in healing He said, Sins forgiven, this may be a curse
Only God forgives sins. Blasphemy. There can be no worse
A Pharisee speaks. 'You can't do that. You can't forgive sin'
Jesus looks at him then the man just healed he has a big grin
'Don't they know what you did?' Peter, is it easier to say
Your sins are forgiven, or take up your bed and walk away?

Jesus teaches his followers patiently letting His words sink in
He wants no more Rome for them, but He wants no more sin
One evening on a hill He teaches a crowd Our Lord's Prayer
It seems so easy. They can pray like this anytime, anywhere
These people are now brimming with hope, spiritual rebirth
To the Pharisees this Jesus is more trouble than He is worth
Daytime, in Galilee, Rome has called all the Jews into court
They are to pay taxes to Rome, these taxes offend and extort
The cruel men who collect them for Rome are all other Jews
Under the Roman yoke of tyranny they tax scorn and bruise

One tax collector there Jesus just stares at, his name is Levi
There was something, a quickening a flaming, in Jesus' eye
Follow me, says Jesus. Where he was a tax collecting Jew
Levi becomes a follower disciple and will be called Matthew

Wait, wait, I say. It is I Nicodemus, your Temple Pharisee
Please tell me now what is it from which all you people flee.'
'Jesus taught outside the temple. We sat with Him all day
The Chief Priests brought a woman, afraid, we ran away.'
'Teacher we all know this woman in adultery she was caught
Jesus, you know the Law of Moses under which we're taught
Says that this adulterous woman we are all to throw stones
Stones pierce her flesh tear her sinews break all her bones.'
'Yes, Jesus, Law of Moses states she must be stoned to death
Struck with these very stones until she takes her last breath.'
'We Chief Priests found her to be adulterous on this day.
All of us here in the Temple want to know what do you say?'
Look Jesus here at the foot of us, stoops down on the sand
And see he is writing something with the finger of his hand
'Can't he hear us talking? Or hear what we've been saying?
We want Jesus to tell us what penalty she should be paying
Under Law of Moses we're given a most grievous command
When a woman is found adulterous she alone must stand
And having given voice to our verdict and making it known
Each Priest and each Pharisee, you're to pick up your stone.'
I Jesus say to each one here who among you is without sin?
Let that man come to take his stone. Be the first to begin.
'Wait, see this Jesus once bend his knee and stoop down.'
'Let us see, he seems to be writing once more on the ground.'
'One Pharisee, dropped his stone. He's willingly departed.'
'And another dropped his too. Look at what Jesus started.
Look there from one Chief Priest another stone just dropped
They've left. All condemnation all fault finding has stopped.'
Woman and where might all those who accused you be
As I look up, I ask has no one here condemned thee?

'No one, Lord, my accusers are gone, left and went away.'
Neither do I condemn you there's no reason for you to stay.
These Priests and Pharisees brought you up to death's door
But now that you are alive and well you may go, sin no more.
Now to all you Pharisees and Chief Priests, to everyone here,
I say I'm the light of the world, follow me and stay near
You'll live the fullest life of faith lit by truth's brightest light
You'll never walk in darkness, you will never fear the night.
'You make claims about yourself, all you say you say of you
Make claims by yourself for yourself saying what is untrue.'
Is it not written in law of Moses that if two witnesses agree
You must accept what they say, I say this law applies to me
I, one witness, say the words my Father allows me to make
My Father who is the second witness He speaks for my sake.
'We are all looking around and we are all now trying to see.
Where's your Father? This Father. Were might He be?'
If you saw signs of my love in this world it is me you knew
When you saw the signs of love you'd know my Father, too.
'You officers of the Temple grab Jesus. Seize this wild man!'
'We are trying to catch him. We're trying as hard as we can

This Jesus where is he? Where's he gone? He was just here.'
'He made himself vanish! How could he just disappear?'
'Wait, there He is now. He's just appeared in another place.'
'Grab Him! Take him. Seize him. Don't give up the chase.'
'What is he gone again? Yes, gone again gone again. Fled.'
'Where is he now? I see him now, he is over there instead.'
I tell you I'm going away, you will search, look, but not find
You shall die in your sins since you have all been long blind
You haven't listened to me when I told you where I am from
When I do go there it'll be a place where you cannot come.
'Can't go where he's to go does this mean himself he'll kill?'
You're from this world and I am not. It is my Father's will.
That is why I said you will die in your sins, that is what I see
You will all die, die in your sins if you do not believe in me.

'Just who are you? You've a strange uniqueness certainly.'
I'm what I've been saying from beginning with certainty.
I tell you there's so much about myself I've yet to announce
In my care there's much to condemn, much to denounce
I have many things to say I have many ways to judge of you
I will always say this one thing, that He who sent me is true.
'Who is this man Jesus is speaking of? What does he attest?'
When you lift up the Son of Man, then you will be blessed.
You shall know who sent Me it is with Him I shall always be
You'll always know that He who sent Me is always with Me.
'We're not Priests or Pharisees as Israelites we're simple kin
Let's kneel before this our Jesus let's not hold fast to sin.'
To you good and so simple people who kneel before me say
It is My Father gives life eternal if My teachings you'll obey
Then you'll all be my disciples and you'll see the truth in Me
That's when you'll know truth. The truth will set you free.
'We are Priests, Pharisees, we come from Abrahams seed
We are born free and we are free, for you we have no need
You say 'You will be made free' yet slaves we've never been.'
I, Jesus, tell you truth that everyone who sins is a slave of sin
I speak to you, I speak to you with words my Father gave
Son of the Father belongs to His family, but not so the slave
The Son's set you free then you'll know you have been freed
It is what the Father tells the Son to do, it is truly so indeed
I know you're from Abraham's seed yet me you try to kill
I follow the will of my Father, you follow your father's will
I've told you the message of my Father, it's not in your heart
It's your father he tells you just what to do where to start.
'A Priest's heart belongs to Abraham, Abraham our father
We Pharisees say the same, why does it cause such bother?'
If you had been Abraham's children you'd do what he did.
Now you seek to murder me, of me you're trying to be rid.
Man who told you what God told Me, man who told you true
Abraham did nothing like this. Your father's deeds you do.
'It is our knowledge of Abraham that we have all mastered.

To say that he is not our father make each of us a bastard.
You're making us angry. We say it's your heart that's hard
We tell you Priests and Pharisees have just one Father-God.'
If God was your Father you'd love Me for from Him I came
But you are the children of your father, the Devil, very same.
From the first, the beginning he was a murderer and a liar
The father of all lies. Blood, red wicked, he flashes forth fire.
Who convicts me of sin? Who wound's me with sin's shame?
I tell true. Believe me when I say that it's from God I came.'
'You are making us angrier still. We know what we must do.
We're right, you're a Samaritan and have a demon in you!'
I have no demon. It is My Father I honor, you dishonor me.
I seek not my own honor, there's One who judges what I see
I tell you whoever obeys my teaching will never die.
'Now we know you've a demon! Away from you all will fly.
Abraham, the prophets died. Having not blood nor breath
You say anyone who keeps Your word will never taste death.
Abraham and the Prophets died all greater than thee.
We ask you Jesus just who do you make yourself out to be?'
I don't honor Myself, it is My Father who does honor to Me.
'One you say is your God, that's what you claim Him to be.'
You've never known Him, I know Him. All that I say is true
Were I to say I don't know Him I would be a liar like you.
I do know Him. I obey His word. I do all that He says to do
Abraham rejoiced to see My time. Father Abraham knew
When he saw My time had come he was not angry or sad
Yes, when I saw your Father Abraham, I saw he was glad.
'You're not yet fifty years old, you have seen Abraham?'
Most assuredly I say to you that before Abraham was I am.
'You were before Abraham is something we cannot discuss.
It is impossible you knew Abraham. You are here with us.
All you Chief Priests and Pharisees take up your stones
Ones we planned to use on the woman to break her bones
Anyone who says they knew Abraham can only displease us
Take up your stones hurl and throw them at this man Jesus.'

'Wait he is gone again so quickly. He is gone. Where now?'
'He's no longer to be seen, disappeared vanished somehow!'

Incense rises in the synagogue it is Sabbath in all the land
Jesus steps into the door finds a man with a withered hand
Is it lawful to heal on the Sabbath, to save a life or to kill?
Jesus heals the man's claw the crowds gasps there's a thrill
'How dare you!' Pharisee, as if He's done something unclean
The healed man is shown not to praise Jesus but to demean
All of this agitation soon in the streets begins to cause a riot
Roman soldiers are only too happy to violently enforce quiet
It is here the Pharisees plot to kill Jesus as tensions mount
And it is here that God will hold these Pharisees to account
The Roman banner has been hung in the Jewish Holy House
Made all the Jews bold to quarrel and right to stir and rouse
1000's gather in Caesarea, Pontius Pilate's home, to protest
He orders banners removed. Of him they've gotten the best

Jesus is now where you do not hear the wheels of the chariot
This is where He will meet the new disciple, Judas Iscariot

At dusk Jesus and His apostles walk up against a steep hill
Below thousands upon thousands in the valley came to fill
And with a prayer and only two fish and five loaves of bread
It was from Jesus these thousands upon thousands are fed

Now Jesus made his Disciples send all the multitudes away
They got into a boat while He went up to a mountain to pray
Jesus goes to them walking on the sea. They cry out in fear
It is I; do not be afraid. Says Jesus. Be of good cheer!

Peter says, 'Lord just command on this water I will stand.'
Come. Peter steps on the water and holds out his hand
Then waves pull him down he yells save me with a shout
Peter, He says, Oh, you of little faith. Why did you doubt?
Back into the boat He makes the wind stop blowing so hard
They all praise him saying, 'Truly You are the Son of God.'

It was Mary whose brother Lazarus was sick
And their sister Martha said Jesus come quick
Now Jesus loved Mary He loved Martha, too
But Jesus loved Lazarus more than anyone knew
When Jesus came Lazarus was four days dead
Your brother shall rise. Is what Jesus said
Mary brought Jesus to where Lazarus was kept
And when Jesus saw Lazarus's death Jesus wept
Jesus thanked his Father then cried with a shout
Lazarus, Lazarus, Lazarus, Lazarus, come out!
Lazarus lay tied and wrapped in grave cloth
But when he heard Jesus, Lazarus came forth
Jesus looked at Lazarus whom he loved so
Untie him, He told them. And let him go.
The Glory of God their fearful eyes shall now behold and see
Christ has conquered death itself for He has set Lazarus free
For Jesus said, It is life, and it is love I give.
Though he be dead, yet shall he rise and live.

It is the week before Passover in Jerusalem, a very holy day
Jesus enters on a donkey. There's palm branches on His way
All the people there are filled with such zeal and such zest
Why? They knew Jesus is coming. That's what they guessed
Priests, Pharisees knew too, waiting for Him to arrive
All will be most fortunate if Jesus leaves Jerusalem alive

So many heads gathered there. Too many to be counted
Look! Look, here He comes. On small donkey He's mounted
People are taking palm branches and laying them at His feet
All these faces calling out to Jesus, wanting to talk and greet
All the people treading a path for Jesus on a sandy savanna
All of Jerusalem comes out to meet Him shouting "Hosanna"
Many were with Him when called Lazarus out of his tomb
So many on this Jerusalem road there's hardly any room
Jesus is so revered by all these people by them He is adored
They're crying blessed is He comes in the name of the Lord
Listen throughout Jerusalem you can hear their voices ring
He rides a lane the crowd calls out Blessed is Israel's King
There are so many more people here just to give Him praise
So many here who love him. Will it be like this always?

'We Pharisees say you Chief Priests haven't done a thing.
They're praising Jesus all day you still hear their voices ring.
We see how in adoration in the people's eyes this man shines
This man Jesus certainly performs many miraculous signs.'

More are celebrating. There has never been such elation
It seems that Jerusalem is witnessing a coronation
They keep following him as He rides along on that small ass
People still laying palm branches before them as they pass

Jesus cuts a tree limb Peter asks, 'What are you making?'
It is a whip, Peter, with it I am going set this temple shaking
You moneychangers listen to me I know what you're about!
Uncharitable, blaspheming, God cursing rogues, get out!
It's where the good people of Israel come to worship to pray.
You've befouled your oaths. Take all things for sale away!
'Rabbi, what are you doing? You've overthrown each table!'
Yes, I am, Peter, I'm making sure that they'll never be able

To buy to sell I am making sure that each one here leaves
See they've turned My Father's House into a den of thieves!

'I'm Nicodemus, a Temple Pharisee, we've heard of you.
You're Jesus of Nazareth, we've heard of the things you do.
Temple moneychangers you say you've the power to dismiss.
What miracle do you do to show you've the right to do this?'
Destroy the temple I will raise it up again in three days.
'46 years to build that short time the Temple you'll raise?'

'Rabbi, it is I alone, Nicodemus, I come to see you once more
We know You come from God our God the God we adore
We know no one could do the wondrous things you do
Unless our God, our God of Abraham, was there with you.'
Nicodemus I Jesus, say to you now, as I said to you then
To see God's Kingdom I say to that you must be born again.
'Can man be again born if brought into life in his prime
Can man enter his mother's womb to be born a 2nd time?'
Again Nicodemus, you must listen to what I say and hear it.
You enter God's Kingdom by being born of water and Spirit
Words that I give you they are words that are new and fresh
That which is born, begotten of the flesh, will always be flesh
Now I am telling you yet again once more so you can hear it
Remember that which is born of Spirit shall always be Spirit
If I say you must all be born again you mustn't be surprised
Holy Spirit may come to you in ways that may be disguised
Hear sound wind makes when the wind blows where it will
May come from the mighty sea or come from the highest hill
I know to the Kingdom of God you are already foresworn
I tell you it is like that with every one of the Spirit born.
'Rabbi, with every one Spirit born? What does that mean?
Tell me how do I begin to believe in what I have never seen?

And what or whose kingdom? And in what or whose land?
I am a Pharisee. I know written law. I do not understand.
I hear all these things that you have thus far said to me
I must bid you to allow me to ask how can these things be?'
You tell how the Holy Spirit sweetly and aptly sings
You a teacher of Israel yet still you don't know these things.
Most assuredly I say to you, we speak of that which we know
With a rhapsody of words we have made Heaven's face glow
It is with these words that we testify about what we've seen
They are the fruits of faith, you don't know what they mean
Still you do not receive and do not follow our true witness
A Pharisee a follower of the written law you lack all fitness
I've told you the earthly parts of things, you do not believe
You've still a spiritual journey ahead that you can't conceive
Now if you are lacking in the highest spiritual quintessence
How'll you ever believe when I tell you of heaven's essence?'

Small home in Jerusalem Peter and Judas knock on the door
And Judas asks Peter, 'What does Jesus want us for?'
Mary Magdalene opens the door welcomes them steps aside
'Everyone's upstairs.' 'Fine,' says Peter, as they step inside
Upstairs Judas says they're blessed to hear all Jesus has said
Blessed they're to be together with Him here to break bread
Yes it is so good that since our Jesus has become so great
When throughout Israel He is the one they celebrate.

Wait, Jesus is rising from the table. Food He has yet to taste
He has taken a towel and He ties the towel around his waist
Now He is pouring water into a basin. What is He up to?
He's walking towards us now who knows what next He'll do
He is so kindly, carefully washing Disciple Nathaniel's feet
He turns to Peter who steps forth, the two of them now meet
'Lord you are washing my feet. I can never allow it to be so.'
Peter, you have no idea what I am doing, later you will know

'But you shall never wash my feet I can never allow it to be.'
Peter, know unless I wash you, you could be no part of Me
'Lord don't wash just my feet wash my hands, my head too.'
Those who bathe are clean you are clean save for one of you
Lord, You've washed our feet, You have given them a sheen
But not all of you. There's still Judas whose feet I must clean
Now do you My Disciples know what I did to you tonight
You call me Teacher and Lord, so I am what you say is right
Now I wash your feet you should wash the feet of everyone
I've given you an example that you should do as I have done
Look see John put his head on Jesus' shoulder as he speaks
A true act of love. John feels the Lord's love that he seeks
I know the ones chosen. I am not talking about all of you
But what it says in Scriptures, all that it says must come true
They say, 'The man who ate with me has turned against me!'
I'm telling you this before it happens before any of it you see
When it happens you'll believe, your belief will set you free
I tell you anyone who receives my messengers receives me
Anyone receives Me receives the One who sent Me to thee
You have called me Lord this is right to do
But I am just a servant to my father and to you
This is what I mean you're now completely clean
For if I did not wash thee thou could not be with me
Know what I have done to you
I have cleansed you through and through
Now confess your sin and you will be forgiven
And he that receives me receive him that sent me

Jesus seems troubled in spirit, something is besetting Him
Peter thinks He surely does. Something is upsetting Him
Truly truly I say unto you by one of you I shall be betrayed.
Who is he speaking of? We should ask Him. We're afraid
Wait, we see Disciple John who's still reclining at Jesus' side
Maybe John will ask if he's not too much in awe or terrified

Lord, who is it? Who could do a thing so traitorous and vile?
It is he I give this dipped bread to you shall know in a while
He is dipping the bread, Peter. Yes, I see Andrew, I see
He is giving it to Judas. Judas is taking it. This can't be!
We are all surprised. Wait, quiet, listen, Jesus speaks
What you do Judas, do quickly. Act, do as your desire seeks
Peter, Judas is hurrying away. He is gone, but where to?
Could he leave Jesus and us like this, how could he dare to?
Who knows where he's gone? And he does hold all our coins
I am sure he'll be buying something in which everyone joins
Did Jesus tell him to see it is delivered, the money released?
Something for the festival beseeming semblance for the feast
I think Jesus was telling him to give some money to the poor
Perhaps, all we know is he took bread, walked out the door
Wait Jesus speaks again. Listen let each word cling to you
Son of Man receives God's glory a glory he'll bring to you
God will bring glory to Him, and God will do it very soon
You'll look for me, not find me from this life I will be hewn
I tell you as I told the people before with all their knowing
I'll be with you little longer, you cannot go where I am going
I and my Father am giving you a commandment that is new
Must love each other, each one love the other, as I love you
Lord where do you go? Share your praise for our Creator
Where I go, Peter, you cannot go, but you will join me later
Lord, why can't I go with you? You know I'd die for thee
Peter before a rooster crows you will three times deny me
This is so unclear. We're his Disciples we should understand
We don't know what he's laying out or what he's planned
Don't be worried! My children, don't have a troubled heart
Have faith in God, have faith in me, this vision I impart
My Father's house has many rooms, I tell you what is true
I am going to my Father's house to prepare a place for you
After I have done this I'll come back to take you all with me
You'll no longer wear the chains of sin and you will be free

You know the way, where I am going. Listen to what I say
Lord, we don't know where, we don't know the way
I am the way the truth and the life this Divine Rule I share
Without me no one can go to the Father this I do declare
If you'd really known me you'd have known Father and all
Henceforth you know him, seen Him, you know His call
Lord show us the Father sufficient unto us it's all we need
I've been with you a long time and yet me you don't heed
Believe I am One with the Father the Father is One with me
Or else have faith in me simply for things I do that you see
If you have faith in me you will be doing the same things I do
I go to Father you'll do greater things than you ever knew
Love me keep my commandments, I'll do all things you ask
Son who brings honor to Father there can be no greater task
They see Judas is back looking in bag making his coins clink
Peter sees he is counting them. 'They are new coins I think.'
Shush, Jesus speaks. Whatever He says we want to hear it
If you love me I'll ask the Father to send you the Holy Spirit
Father's Holy Spirit, my Spirit who will always be with you
Holy Spirit will show you all that is right and all that is true
Other people can't accept Spirit. Him they don't see or know
The Holy Spirit will keep living in you wherever you may go
I won't worry you I won't leave you like an orphan all alone
You'll see me they won't, I'll live in you, it's what I've shown
You'll know I'm One with the Father You're One with me
He'll show what I'm like He'll show you what you too can be
If you keep my commands I'll love you, I'll be one with you
It is the one who loves me who'll be loved by my father too
Lord what is that you mean, he'll show us what you are like
Lord, do you mean all others their hearts You will not strike
Anyone loves me my Father loves them we'll live one place
Those who don't love or believe for them there's no space
Judas counts his coins adding up the full sum in his sack
It as if he has not heard a word since he has been back
Jesus is giving us his words he is speaking once more

46

Listen closely to all he says, over his words they must poor
I've told you things while I am with you, tried to reach you
In my place Father will send the Spirit Who will teach you
Holy Spirit he will remind you of everything here that I said
Love Me, love my words, I must face what is coming ahead
I will leave with you the kind of peace that only I can give
My peace is nothing like the peace this world where you live
I've already said I am going do not be afraid, do not worry
But I'll also come back soon into your hearts I will hurry
If you loved me be glad I am going back celebrate the joy
I go to One greater than I, this world's ruler we will destroy
Lord tell us what you want us to do we'll listen to all you say
Yes we're your Disciples Lord command us, we will obey
Keep all my commandments if you love me
But I give you a commandment that's new
That you love your sister and brother
That you have love for each other
That each one love the other
As I have loved you
My father will love you if you love me
And I will love you too
Ask of my Father in my name
And there's nothing, nothing He won't do
I go to prepare a place for you
Like a husband for a wife
Without me to my father you cannot go
For I am the way the truth and the life
But I will not leave you helpless
I will leave the Holy Spirit who is true
Then you shall know that my father is in me
And I, I am in you
You cannot go where I am going
I would not say it if it were not so
But believe in my Father and in me
And later you shall follow

I tell you this before it happens so when it does you'll believe
When it does happen you'll have faith in me you'll not grieve
Can't speak much more the ruler of this world comes near
But he has no rule over me, this should give you good cheer
I obey my Father, love Him so everyone in the world might
So rise let us go from here come let us together leave this site
Let us all His Disciples follow Peter, Judas has stayed behind
Judas seems well alone. Maybe there is more money to find

But for his disciples The Garden of Gethsemane is deserted
Jesus spent the last hour in prayer that He has asserted
And why is He given to render and pray such holy prayer?
Because He knows the time to leave this world is near
Disciples don't seem anxious about promises they're to keep
For they're all curled up on the garden ground, fast asleep
Spirit is willing, the body is weak. Wake Up! He'll demand
Stay awake, Disciples, stay awake, for the hour is at hand!
My Disciples I say truly that it fits your faith to believe in me
The time is coming it's already here when scattered you'll be
It'll look like I've been left all alone but I will never be alone
I know Father is always with me by the love He has shown
I've told you this so that you might have peace in your heart
The world will make you suffer be brave we will never part
You will all suffer for me for me that is how you'll be treated
But yes I say again be brave for it's the world I've defeated
Wait see, see, Jesus is looks up now to heaven he is gazing
Yes, quiet, listen, to his father he is in prayer and praising
Father hour's come to glorify thy Son so I may glorify Thee
Eternal life is to know You the only true God, to know me
Your Son Jesus who You the supreme loving God has sent
Pray love for those whose love for you has been well spent
I brought glory to You where such creatures as men doubt
Give me the glory we had before world You brought about
Father I am coming to You but my followers are still here
With Your power may we be one together with love so dear

While I was here I guarded them not one did You let be lost
You love them as I love them they are worth pain and cost
One had to be lost so that what Scriptures claim would arise
I know they will be purchased with my life, made your prize
I pronounce these things now before I am on my way to you
So My followers will have the same complete joy that I do
I brought You glory and the work You gave me to do is done
Father I ask keep my followers here safe from the evil one
Your word is truth Father truth opens Your divine doors
It's your truth Father let this truth make them totally Yours
I now send them into the world Father just as You sent me
Now I give Myself completely so they may be completely free
I know Father when I leave my followers will grieve on me
I Pray my leaving will cause those to come to believe on me
You do love them as much as me I pray this they may know
Let everyone You have given me be with me wherever I go
They don't know You, I know there is no world without You
My followers know You sent me. I told them all about you
As our love becomes love for them they will love you more
Treasures of Your love into their thankful hearts You pour
Father the love You have for me will become part of them
Father they and I will be One We'll be in the heart of them
Jesus is praying for me. He prays for me. He prays for us all.
A true prayer, hearing our Lord Jesus to His father call
Jesus prayed to His father He prayed for you and me
He said Father glorify thy Son that thy Son may glorify Thee
Life eternal is to know thee, to know the only God that's true
Father give me glory I had in heaven when I was with You
I pray dear Father for those to come who shall believe on Me
I pray dear Father we all be one as, as I am one with Thee
The glory You gave Me I give to them so they may be in You
They will know that You love them and I will love them too
'Oh Father, we've known You, we know he came from thee.'
May they be with Me to behold my glory, you have given Me

I made your love known, so your love may be in them too
Now I am in them and you love them, as I, as I, love you
'Peter, look here comes Judas, and with him two temple men
Sirs, who do you seek? 'Jesus of Nazareth. you are he then?'
Yes, I am he. Two officers are backing away, stepping aside
Looks like they want to arrest Jesus. They haven't even tried
They've fallen. Look, see, Judas is lifting both on their feet
'Who?' 'This Jesus' I am the one you want to meet.
Now I've told you I am he, I ask you to let these others go.
Peter's sword struck a high priest servant. 'Stop him. No!
'Sheath swords. We mustn't fight. You mustn't even think it
This cup my Father poured out for me shall I not drink it?
They've taken Jesus! They have bound him, taken him away
They've tied his hands, feet. What has Judas done this day?
Jesus is with the Chief Priest. Peter and John are near
They are being very quiet they don't want anyone to hear
John goes in Temple Courtyard Peter waits outside the door
A woman outside the Courtyard says she's seen Peter before
'I think you are one of His Disciples. 'No, woman, I am not.'
Chief Priest talks. Now this Jesus will come to know His lot
'I, Temple Priest ask Jesus of Nazareth, what is your creed?' I've
spoken openly. There's no understanding you need.
In our synagogues Temple that's where my word was caught
You want to know how I came by it, what it is I taught
Our people wherever they gather in their press and throng
I've not said anything in secret I've not said anything wrong
Question me now? Why this rash haste so hurriedly shed?
Ask the people who heard me. They'll tell you what I said.
'You dare to answer that way!' 'That Officer just beat Him!'
'Jesus has fallen to his knees! Oh see how they treat Him!'
'Wait, Jesus speaks. If I've done something wrong say so.
Why hit me when I am here to speak of what I know?
A man with a lantern comes near. He does not look pleased
It was the man who was in the garden when Jesus was seized
Says to Peter were you not in the garden in that very place?

'I was not. I tell you now get the lantern away from my face.'
Then comes a Temple officer with something he wants to say
'You, were you in the garden when we took Jesus away?'
'Jesus? Garden? I was never there. I've no way of knowing.'
Did you hear Peter? As you spoke it was the cock crowing
Peter says, 'My heart is spent, is spent is spent with grief
Oh Lord, Oh Lord, all my strength is lost to my unbelief
Each breath I take is filled with sighs because of my own lies
Lord, how great You are to those who follow, however far
Put Your love in my heart give me the courage again to start
Dear Lord bow down Your ear listen to this humble prayer
Enemies trample trod, should've trusted you you're my God
Could've stood me on 2 feet given me strength foes to meet
Please take back all they stole please reach down in my soul
God I call out Your Name why not before? I feel such shame
Vicious threats put me in shock, this from Peter, your rock
Hide me from questions sprung take away this lying tongue
Hide me in your secret place shower me with Your grace
Oh Lord how can it be? How could I have denied thee?
Oh Lord can You forgive? Must I go on? How can I live?
Lord Oh Lord You now must die. And all I did was to deny
My moment of truth. So weak. Lost all faith. Couldn't speak

Jesus stands in the Judgment Hall with a Temple escort
It is with grief and sorrow that He is brought to the court
Chief Priests and Pharisees are all here, they are waiting too
They all want to see with this Jesus what Pilate is like to do
There is to be a great reckoning. Now Pilate enters the room
Chief Priests, Pharisees before beginning to rant and fume
'Know I Pontius Pilate serving under the Emperor Tiberius
Ask what are the charges, let's hope it's nothing too serious.'
'He's criminal! We brought Him to your court held in awe.'
'Then take Him yourselves, judge him by your own law.'
'Pontius Pilate we Chief Priests say til we're scant of breath
That Moses Law does not allow us to put any man to death.'

'Then let me ask the prisoner, are you the King of the Jews?'
Asking on your own, or did another give you this news?
'I'm no Jew! If it's a Jewish leader you seek I'm not the one.
The leaders brought you here. So tell us what've you done?
My kingdom is not of this world, it is from another place
If it were, then my followers have fought and given chase
keep me from being handed over you would they overwhelm
now my kingdom does not belong here it is not of this realm
'A king?' You say correctly. For this reason was I born
And against false traitors to my kingdom I've come to warn
I came into the world to speak truth that even you shall see
Belong to the truth for who belongs to truth belongs to me
'I ask you, what is truth?' 'Look they bring in another man.'
'The Chief Priests say we're to help them if we can.'
'They have brought that bound man to stand at Jesus' side.'
'Pilate speaks. Priests tell us by his words we must bide.'
'I Pontius Pilate say I find no fault in the man Jesus at all
You have a Jewish custom here so to you people I am to call
I must give someone at Passover. My words will be brief
Do I release the King of the Jews? Or Barabbas this thief?'
'No, not this man, but Barabbas, listen to the others shout.
People are calling for Barabbas, can there be any doubt?'

They put Jesus on his knees and tie his wrists around a post
The Temple Officers' pleasing task is to whip Jesus the most
Whip Him again! Ha! Jesus is theirs for this bloody hour
Crown of thorns, tattered cloak, ask where be your power
See how he winces in pain, they'll show him pain that's true
'Hail, King of the Jews! That is who you are. A king, a Jew!'
'Who needs a whip?' 'There! I have hit You with my hand!'
'I do the same Ha! King of Jews we serve at your command!'

Pilate calls the Chief Priests to show what he is going to do
Here's Pilate. 'I, Pontius Pilate will bring Him out to you.

People of Jerusalem you see that in Him I find no crime
You Temple Officers bring this Jesus out for one last time.'
See a crown of thorns and in a purple robe he is cloaked
Look how badly His body's beaten how in blood He's soaked
He's fallen to his knees. 'I, Pilate, say behold the Man! See!'
We people all say crucify him! You mustn't let him go free
'I say to you people, this matter has now come to a halt.
Take and crucify Him for in Him I do not find any fault.'
'We've a law in our well-ordered nation on our sacred sod
To our holy law He's to die who claims to be the Son of God.
'Son of God? Something troubling, disturbing goes on here
This something dangerous and admit my thoughts of fear
Ask Him myself follow me back to the Judgement Hall come
Jesus, I, Pilate, Prefect want to know where are you from?'
Jesus' still on his knees, his head his bowed, he is in pain
He does not answer. 'Jesus, answer. I will make this plain
I say to you that I can crucify you or I can let you go free.'
God gave you this power or you could do nothing to me
My father I love truth I love, sworn to it I have always been
The one who handed me over to you is guilty of a greater sin
'Officers, untie this man's hands and make him stand!
Now I'm taking you to the people of Jerusalem as planned.'
'People say if you let this Man go, you're not Caesar's friend
Crucify Him you'll do your best service to Caesar in the end.
Kingship claims go against Caesar this Pontius Pilate knows
Chief Priest knew these people listened, Pilate they oppose

Pilate walks Jesus back. His Prefect chair Pilate will preside
How badly beaten this Jesus is. He has a soldier on each side
Pilate is going to speak. 'People of Jerusalem see your king.'
People of Jerusalem say away with Him! He deserves dying!
Away with him! Crucify him! 'Your King I should crucify?'
'We have no king but Caesar! This false messiah must die!'

'People of Jerusalem you've spoken there's nothing I can say
Soldiers here's prisoner Jesus. I order you take him away!'

They came to see that to the cross Jesus has been nailed
And He has. The Priests and Pharisees plans have not failed
Along with two thieves one on each side, Jesus is in between
The crowd looks on. The day of His death will finally be seen
Look how he bows down His head. His torment, pain is clear
On the other side, four women. What are they doing here?
Jesus' mother, Martha, Mary who might that 4th woman be?
Mary Magdalene another Jesus follower who did not flee
Look, there standing with them isn't that His Disciple John?
Yes he's looking on in great sorrow, they all watch on and on
Here comes Pilate. He's holding something. A piece of cloth
He put it above Jesus. What for? What's he bringing forth?
Says JESUS OF NAZARETH THE KING OF THE JEWS
'Pilate, I Chief Priest say those are wrong words you choose.
Don't write, 'King of the Jews' but that's what he claimed
'What I've written I've written.' The Priests feel ashamed
Pilate leaves Officer in charge takes Jesus's garment away
Garment shows no sign of His sufferings. It is bright as day
'It has no seam. Rip it now, give half to you and half to me.'
'Let's not tear it but cast dice for it to see whose it shall be.'
'Here is my lucky dice roll!' 'Now the dice are mine to throw
I win. We're leaving. I'll take the garment with me as we go.
The 4 women and the Disciple John now approach the cross
They look so sad. They know and show the very heart of loss
See Mary His mother, hard misfortune begets tears she cried
See there at the cross is disciple John is standing at her side
Jesus speaks Mary His mother. 'Woman behold your son!'
'Behold your mother' They knew before his words begun

Jesus is suffering, surely he will soon breathe his last breath
The Pharisees are here to witness his suffering and death

Jesus thirsts. An officer reaches into a pot, brings a sponge
He rubs it roughly on Jesus' mouth. A vinegar wet plunge
Jesus stares at the sky. It is finished! Is He dead? Almost.
See He is bowing His head down. He is giving up the ghost
Lord into your hands I commit
My heart, soul, My spirit'
For when He gave His Spirit to You
That's when He gave You our Spirit too

Pilate, I am Joseph Arimathea. I am Nicodemus a Pharisee
I know you. Joseph you were a follower? That is new to me
I kept it secret. When Jesus asked me to follow him I tried it
Now that Jesus is dead and gone, there is no reason to hide it
Nicodemus, you too? I visited Jesus once and he made me see
Once was all it took? Well, now tell, what do you want of me
We take Jesus' body it's not stealing we will not be accused
We'll lay His body in my tomb nearby it's never been used
We've linen cloth to wrap the body in it is what we prefer
I have fetched precious spices made from aloes and myrrh
It is accepted you Jewish people bury your dead in that way
Sabbath is coming and so we want to take Jesus' body today
Give you leave to take the body of Jesus down from his cross
I must ask you to forgive me if I do not weep for your loss

Peter, John early morning brought dim darkness and gloom
A fair pair of heels I went running to our Lord Jesus' tomb
Tomb was empty. It was desolate, deserted, abandoned, bare
They've taken carried away our Lord, we know not where
John run to tomb to see if what Mary Magdalene says is true
Let's run from here and run there now. And I'm coming, too

What's in the tomb, It is empty. Peter, is it what I feared?
Yes save for linen wrapping, a head cloth the tomb's cleared

Oh, I do weep for our Jesus. Woman, why are you weeping?
My Lord is gone. I do not know where him they are keeping
Woman, whom are you seeking? Why are you crying
Sir, if you have carried Him away, tell me where he is lying
Mary! Rabbi! Touch me not, to my father I am not ascended
Go to my brethren, say unto them, that nothing has ended
Lord, you astound me, I'm stunned, amazed, overawed
I ascend to my Father, your Father to my God and your God

Here we are. Jesus' Disciples. All come together, side by side
Save for Thomas. He still feels the risk, and he wants to hide
Without zeal and love of our Jesus, what we should do now
I think we should try to stay together. But I don't know how
Stay together? Jesus is gone. So is what is the reason
I do know without the Rabbi here things seem out of season
Wait, that light there? So clear, so shining, so close. See?
I see it. What is it? Reason cannot compass what it can be?
It is Jesus! Are you sure? Look at His wounded hands
He is pointing to the wound at his side. Before us He stands
Peace be with you. Lord, we're so glad so glad to meet thee
It is with the greatest delight, the greatest joy we greet thee
Quiet, listen to our Jesus speak, our master, our friend, too
Peace be with you. As the Father has sent me I also send you
Receive Holy Spirit. If you forgive the sins they'll be quelled
If you hold a man's sins all past all to come, they'll be held

Thomas, we have seen the Lord, from death he is free
I tell you and I tell all the Disciples that first I must see
Woeful wounds in his flesh in his hands the print of the nails
Unless I thrust my hands into his side on me your story fails
Thomas, but we have seen him, this we are telling you
I repeat Peter, that I very deeply doubt what you say is true
Peter, Thomas, everyone, it's here again. That shining light
Rays and beams. It is like the sun of heaven shining bright

A dream? But we're awake. Look at Jesus stand and walk
No dream. Behold our Lord Jesus. Wait he's about to talk
Peace to you. Thomas here on my hands let a finger thrust
Put your hand in my side. Stop doubting Thomas, and trust
My Lord, my God I thought I'd never see you again never
Now that I've seen my Lord, My God I'll have faith forever
Thomas you have faith just because your eyes have seen me
But blessed be them who've faith in what their eyes don't see

No fish. There's nothing to be got. Do we fish for them?
Draw your nets up and cast them. Let us wish for them
Been throwing these nets from the side of our boat all day
Now it's night, still nothing, no fish. Perhaps we should pray
Draw them up, Philip and cast them again, Peter, once more
See isn't that someone standing upon the edge of our shore?
Who is it Nathaniel? He calls to us. Not certain who it is yet
Children, have you any food? We don't. We've an empty net
Cast the net on the right side of the ship, some you shall find
We might as well do what the stranger says just to be kind
Yes, Peter, now look, Peter, look, our net is filled with fish
I see, cast again, this is more than our desires can wish
And again, again, with fish the net is filled to overflowing
Yes, how could that man on shore be so very knowing
What joy at having caught all this fish we can only rejoice
Yes John how could that man on shore make the right choice
Peter, look! See who it is who told us where our nets to toss
Who is it, John? I see is a man on shore with his arms across
It is the Lord. Look Peter dove in. He's swimming to land
Peter is there already. See where he and the Lord stand
Let's row back as fast as we can. Look, there is Jesus now
I see him, sitting by the fire, just sitting there somehow
He is calling to us again. Bring the fish you've just caught
Lord our net is filled. We'll bring all that may be brought
Come together we shall eat, together we will break the fast
Breaking bread with our Lord may this time never be past

Simon son Jonah do you love me more than these others do
Lord you know I do love you even more than my brothers do
Feed my lambs. Simon, son of Jonah I ask do you love Me
Lord you know that I love you with a love as great as can be
Feed my sheep Your sheep Simon son Jonah do you love Me
Lord makes me sad when you ask me 3 times if I love thee
You who know all things must know how dearly I love you
Feed my sheep Peter, I am telling you what's true
When you were young you used to go anywhere you desired
When old you'll stretch out your hands you'll be dull, tired
You shall live this day, see old age see much than you know
You'll end up tied up and taken where you do not want to go
What does that mean, John? I know the subject of his story
Jesus talks about the way which you will die, give God glory
Follow Me. What about this man John what'll he be to Thee
If I want him to live til I come what is that to you Follow me
To my Father I am leaving be not faithless but believing
The Holy Spirit You are receiving
Peace be with you peace with you
It is I that you are looking at do not doubt what you see
You've found what you are seeking you have found it in me
In me you have the power the power to do the most
Now baptize in the name of the father Son and Holy Ghost

Peter has been radically changed by God's saving grace
He miraculously makes a lame beggar stand up in place
The beggar with a smile for first in his life is able to stand
The crowd rejoicing chants this was done by Jesus's hand

So many followers since Peter gave lame man legs new lease
That Pharisee Caiaphas knew these followers had to cease

Pilgrims stop to hear disciple Stephen preaching on a street
Despite threats by Caiaphas they will still go there to meet
'Jesus to forgive sin was crucified but rose from the dead'
The crowd hangs on every word and all that Stephen said
'Impossible,' cries Saul. A rough tough intellectual Pharisee
Stephen will be martyred Christians to Damascus will flee

To follow and catch them Saul takes the Damascus Road
He will kill any Christian there whose face dare showed
Suddenly as he's riding, around Jesus shines a brilliant light
'Who are you?' Saul hits the ground, all eyes and no sight
Why do you persecute me? Jesus asks. 'Who are you?'
Tries look away could not turn his eyes from immortal view
I am Jesus, whom you persecute. 'No! No! No! No! No!'
Paul is blinded by the light. This is what Jesus did bestow

In the name of Father Son and Holy Spirit gone now is Saul
Apostle who'll share Good News about Jesus name is Paul

Romans against Christians ready to do further dark deeds
Behead disciple James as caution to all followers it succeeds
Disciples will spread God's word making hearts climb
Changing religious culture one believer, one soul at a time

Peter's travels to Jewish communities he is prone
It is tiring work. He has never felt so alone
In his work he brings the first Roman Cornelius to Jesus
By doing this Peter knew Abraham and God he pleases

But its Paul who takes the Word to the empire so very hard
Paul who once tried to crush those who thought Jesus is God
Paul: No longer Jew or Greek, male or female, slave or free
We're one in Christ. World changing words as world will see

Peter is crucified, and Paul is beheaded, both in Rome
All the other disciples who knew Jesus, heaven is their home
John's the last disciple standing. Exiled to a remote isle
Jesus comes to John in visions and John writes all the while
One thing he wrote while there, this is just one sample
Book of Revelation, the last book of the Bible for example:
Greetings,
A revelation of Jesus Christ of what must soon take place
Sending it through His angel to servant John, before his face
Favored is he reads this prophecy for time's come round
John, to 7 Asian churches and Spirits before God's crown
And from Jesus Christ who loves and freed us from our sins
To Him be glory, power forever and always, eternity begins
Look, He is coming with the clouds! Every eye shall see
I am Alpha Omega one who is, was, is coming, the Almighty
I John cause of my witness about Jesus we share endurance
Behind me loud voice trumpet like Spirit inspired assurance
Saying Write in a book send to seven churches in the lands
I saw the voice speaking to me and 7 golden lampstands
Stood son of man long robe golden girdle wondrous attire
Head and hair white as snow eyes were like a flame of fire
Feet like burnished bronze, voice like many waters rushing
His hand held 7 stars his face was sun full strength blushing
I fell at his feet. I'm the first and the last, Fear not be brave
I'm alive forever. I have the keys of Death and the Grave
Write down what you've seen and all your further searches
As for the 7 stars and 7 lampstands they are the 7 churches
Write to the church in Ephesus and so I command
The words of the one who holds the 7 stars in his right hand
'I know what you are doing. You work hard and long.
You can't put up with those who are evil and do wrong.
You have tested those who claim to be apostle but are not.
You've found out that they are liars. They shall be caught.
You have shown endurance for me and never did you thirst
I've this against you you've let go of the love you had at first'

Remember then from what you have fallen I say here repent
If not, I will remove your lampstand from you, torn and rent
But you have this in your favor and in you full weight
You hate what the Nicolaitans are doing, which I also hate.
Eat from tree of life God's paradise you who conquer strife
The words of the first the last who was dead, came to life:
I know your poverty though by Me you're actually enriching
I know all that's been said about you by Satan's bewitching
Fear not. You'll be imprisoned. I know who lives, who dies
You will win the victory. A 2nd life will by your prize
The one with the sharp two-edged sword this message I tell
Know where you live there where Satan has his throne in hell
You are true to me you gave your faith to me, all that it gives
When Antipas faithful witness was killed where Satan lives
I have things against you, you taught Balaam's reaching's
In the same way, some who follow Nicolaitans' teachings
Change your hearts or I will come soon, make war, believe it
There'll be a white stone new name for those who receive it
These are words of God's Son from whose eyes fire just pour
I know your love, and faithfulness, even greater than before

But I have something against you: Jezebel, there it begins
I gave her time she refuses to turn away from her sexual sins
All those who sin with her will suffer unless they turn away
Searching each heart I'll reward for what was done each day
If you don't know Satan's secrets, or know where he's from
I Jesus say, Just hold on to what you have until I come.
I give authority to where those people choose to live and stay
To rule the nations with an iron rod and smash them like clay
I received from my Father so I give them the morning star.
If you can hear, listen to what the Spirit is saying so far
Write this to the angel of Sardis of the whole parish church
God's 7 spirits of the 7 stars know your works you besmirch
Wake up, strengthen yourself, you are near your last breath
You are teetering on the brink of absolute disgraceful death

For in God's eyes I've found your works far from complete
Such behavior you know your Savior you could never meet
Remember what you've heard. Change your lives and hearts
Or I'll come a thief in the night to break you into 1000 parts
But you do have some whose clothing has not been stained
They'll walk with Me because my blessing they have gained
Those who emerge victorious wear white clothing like this
In the scroll of life with my Father and his Angels, what bliss
Hear, listen, you know it is God's will you must be obeying
This is God's Holy Spirit, to the churches that He is saying
To the angel of the Philadelphia Church this you are to write
The words of David's key opens or shuts it stays locked tight
I know your works. In front of you a door no one can shut
With little power My word you have always refused to cut
I will make those from Satan's synagogue before you bow
I'll make them realize that I love you, I made a heavenly vow
Because you my lawful command you kept, you must endure
I will keep you safe when the earth is tested this I assure
I am coming soon for the glory and success of my conquest
Hold on to what you have so that no one takes your crest
Whose Father's hand shall emerge great proud, victorious
Make them pillars in the temple of God it will be glorious
I'll write them on New Jerusalem, write them in God's name
I'll write them in my new name giving them all-telling fame
Then pray I say to thee, you must, you will, you shall hear it
Churches all churches I say to you listen, listen, to the Spirit
Laodicea's church Angel, God's creation a faithful witness
I know your works. Neither cold nor hot. There is no fitness
Because you're lukewarm neither hot nor cold, you are unfit
Out of my mouth and tongue it is you that I am about to spit
You say you're rich, wealthy these are delusions of grandeur
You don't know you're miserable blind naked pathetic poor
My advice is buy gold from me it's purified and transposed
Be rich in white clothing your nakedness won't be exposed
There be an ointment on your eyes so that you may see

I correct those I love. Change their hearts. Make them free
I'm standing at the door knocking. Open it and you shall see
I will have dinner with them. They will have dinner with me
Those who are victorious they sit with my Father the king
Just as I sat with my Father. It was and is a glorious thing
Then pray I say to thee, you must, you will, you shall hear it
Churches all churches I say to you listen, listen, to the Spirit
After this I looked there had been in heaven an opened door
First voice I heard sounding like a trumpet began to pour
'Come up here, I will show you what must now take place.'
I saw a throne in heaven someone seated on it in that space
The one seated there looked like jasper, carnelian all aglow
Around the throne was emerald that looked like a rainbow
From the throne came lightning voices, thunder from heaven
Flaming torches, spirits of God, their number was seven
Crystal was in front of the throne, something like a glass sea
Four living creatures encircled the throne and there they be
Creatures were covered with eyes on the front, on the back
Faith, thought lost, but fear and desperation I did not lack
The 1st creature like a lion the 2nd creature like an ox in sight
The 3rd creature like human the 4th creature an eagle in flight
have 6 wings covered with eyes keep on saying and humming
"Holy is the Lord God Almighty who was, is and is coming."
Glory to the one seated on the throne always and whenever
This given by the living creatures to He who lives forever
24 elders fall worship before He on the throne, these are they
They throw down their crowns before the throne and say
Lord God, by glory and honor, power you have been kissed
you create all things By your will they were created and exist
He on the throne held a scroll before him I wanted to kneel
'Who is worthy to open the scroll, and break its seal?'
But no one in heaven or earth could open it or look inside it
I began to weep cause no one was worthy I couldn't abide it
Lion of Judah, Root of David, elder said 'look, don't weep.'
Standing slain I saw with 7 horns and eyes, a lamb, a sheep

God's 7 spirits sent out to set the whole world on wheels
This is how to emerge victor and open the scroll and 7 seals
He came, took the scroll from the one on the throne seated
4 creatures 24 elders falling before the Lamb he was greeted
Each held a harp and golden bowls full of incense
Which are prayers of the saints, it was most intense
You are worthy to open its seals because you were slain
By your blood purchased persons from every sea and plain
You gave a kingdom, God's priests, removing every chain
Now it is by your purchased blood on earth they will reign
Angels around the throne. Thousands Millions. I'm guessing
They say Worthy is slaughtered lamb honor wisdom blessing
Every creature in heaven, on earth, under it, and in the sea
Say blessing, honor, glory, and power belong always to thee
The one seated on the throne to the Lamb forever and then
The elders worshipped and the 4 living creatures said Amen
The Lamb opened one of 7 seals as I looked on in wonder
I hear one of the creatures say 'Come!' A voice like thunder
A white horse. Rider with a bow, a crown. Just a beginning
Going forth from victory to victory, winning and winning
The Lamb opened the second seal in front of me
I heard the second living creature say, 'Come and see.'
Out came another horse, fiery red rage that failed to cease
Its rider given a large sword from earth will take peace
Lamb opened the 3rd seal. 3rd creature, "Come" Command.
A black horse. Its rider held a pair of scales in his hand.
I heard what sounded like voices from the four living beasts
'A quart of wheat for a day's wages.' At the very least
'And three quarts of barley for a day's wages.' Heavy toil
But do not do damage to the vineyards and the olive oil
Lamb opened the 4th seal. 4th creature, "Come" Appears
Behold a pale horse followed by Hell. Dangers, doubts, fears
Its rider named Death given authority over ¼ of earth to kill
By war, famine, disease, beasts, any blood it may seek to spill
He opened the 5th seal, and it was under the alter that I saw

Souls slain on the account of the word of God, I stood in awe
And they cried, loud voice, How long, O Lord, please tell
Before you avenge our blood on them who on earth do dwell
Each was given a white robe, rest they were told, this is why
Til their fellow servants who like them were about to die
He opened the 6th seal a great earthquake how I fear to tread
Sun turned black as funeral cloth the moon turned blood red
All the number of the stars of the sky to the earth they fell
As a fig drops its fruit when a strong wind is wont to swell
The sky it disappeared like a scroll
As if it were just one piece in a roll
Every high mountain, every fair island in their space
Were removed from there out of their natural place
Then everyone, generals, the powerful, officials in all things
The rich, the slave and the free, crowned and anointed kings
They hid themselves in caves and in the mountain blocks
Then they called out to the mountains and to the rocks
'Fall, hide us from the face of the one seated on the throne
And also from the Lamb's wrath, may we be let alone!
Of a mountain and a rock and a block is this a just demand?
The great day of their wrath has come who is able to stand?
After this I saw at 4 corners of the earth there were angels 4
They held back earth's 4 winds so that they'd blow no more
Another Angel holding God's living seal making a great plea
To the 4 who had been given power to damage earth and sea
Dont harm earth til we've sealed those who serve God's plan
The number sealed: 140,000 sealed from every Israelite clan
From the tribe of Judah, twelve thousand were sealed
From the tribe of Reuben, twelve thousand was the yield
Twelve thousand from the tribe of Gad
Twelve thousand from the tribe of Asher were had
Twelve thousand from the tribe of Naphtali
Twelve thousand from Manasseh was the tally
Twelve thousand From the tribe of Simeon
Twelve thousand from the tribe of Levi were done

Twelve thousand from the tribe of Issachar
Twelve thousand from the tribe of Zebulun so far
Twelve thousand from the tribe of Joseph of such fame
Twelve thousand from the tribe of Benjamin a good name
After this I looked there was a great crowd a great creation
They were from every tribe, people, language and nation
They were standing before the Lamb and the throne
White robes, palm branches in their hands are shown
Crying: 'Victory belongs to our God who on the throne sits.'
'And to the Lamb.' Their glorious love of Both never quits
All the angels now in a circle the throne they've gone round
And the elders the four living creatures they fell facedown
Before the throne and worshipped God, 'Amen', saying
Blessing, glory, wisdom, power, might, to our God,' praying
Then one of the twenty four elders, he spoke to me
'These people wearing white robes from where do they flee?'
I said, 'Sir, you know.' He said, 'They come from the mud.
They've washed their robes made white in Lamb's blood.'
Before God's throne worshipping him and I will tell you why
The one seated on the throne will shelter them where they lie
No hunger or thirst anymore. Water to brim it will drown
Sun or scorching heat on them no longer will beat down
Lamb in the throne's midst will shepherd them from fear
lead to the life-giving water God will wipe away every tear.'
Lamb opened the 7th seal for ½ hour comes silence in heaven
7 angels stand before God what's given to them is trumpets 7
Another angel came burning incense in a golden bowl
Offering before the throne for prayers of saints on a scroll
Yet another angel came and before the altar he did stand
The incense smoke rose up before God from the angel's hand
Angel took the censer filled it with altar fire made it to shake
Threw it to earth came thunder voices lightning earthquake
7 angels who had 7 trumpets prepared themselves to sound
And the sound they choose to make cannot help but astound
1st angel blew his trumpet hail and fire with blood appeared

Was thrown down to the earth, in field and town all feared
All the grass burned up, on and on the hail and fire stirred
The trees, and the very earth was all burned up by a third
The 2nd angel blew his trumpet as it were a mountain great
Fire in the sea. A third is blood. Its strength does not abate
1/3rd of the creatures in the sea died, of life they were devoid
And a 1/3rd of the ships lie wrecked buried and destroyed
And the third angel sounded, and there fell a great star
From heaven, burning as it were a lamp, and it fell far
On a 1/3rd of all springs of water against all nature it delivers
Then burning like a torch it fell on a 1/3rd of all the rivers
The star's name is Wormwood
1/3rd of the waters became wormwood it wasn't very good
Because the water had become so bitter and so sour
Many people died from the water's evil power
4th angel sounded: sun, moon, stars, day, lost a 1/3rd of light
And a 1/3rd of light was also gone from the shades of night
Then I looked and I heard an eagle flying high overhead
'Oh, Horror, horror!' In a loud clear brass voice it said
'Those on earth remaining trumpet blasts they don't know
That the three angels in flames of fire are about to blow!'
Fifth angel sounded a star from heaven fell 'twere not amiss
And it's he that was given the key to the shaft of the abyss
He opened the shaft of the abyss; and up the smoke rose
From the shaft, like a huge furnace all the smoke it throws
Fiery flames, burning smothering smoke did cough and spit
Very sun and air were darkened by the smoke from that pit
Came locusts, they rose with the smoke from the first hour
Unto them given power as scorpions of the earth have power
Told not to hurt the grass or strike any plant or tree dead
But only each man who lacks the seal of God on his forehead
And to them it was given that they should not kill
But that they should torment for five months if you will
Suffering it inflicts like that scorpion when person it stings
Men seek death and shall not find it, shall fly away on wings

The locusts looked like horses ready for all battle tests
On their heads were what seemed to be gold crests
Faces were like human faces and eyes that could outstare
Teeth were like lions' teeth, their hair was like women's hair
And they had breastplates of iron on their chests bracing
Their wings sounded like chariot horses into battle racing
And just like unto scorpions, they had a stinger in their tail
They had over men for 5 months power to hurt and assail
They have a king Abaddon is his Hebrew name
In Greek it is Apollyon, it means the same
He is an angel from the abyss
The 1st horror passed. Look! There come two woes after this
And the 6th angel sounded I heard a voice from the horns 4
Of the golden altar which is before God it did roar
Saying to 6th angel with the trumpet the 4 angels now loose
Who are bound at the river Euphrates don't ask or induce
Four angels made ready released to kill of mankind a third
Cavalry troops two hundred million. Their number I heard
This is the way I saw the horses and their riders in the view
With breastplates that were fiery red sulfur yellow dark blue
Horses' heads were like lions' heads lions no man could tame
And out of their mouths came smoke, and sulfur, and flame
By 3 plagues 1/3 of mankind died out of their mouths it came
Issuing smoke and sulfur and burning unquenchable flame
Power is in their mouths, their tails, they do what it takes
With heads that inflict injuries, for their tails are like snakes
Rest of mankind who by these plagues to hell were not sent
Didn't change their hearts and lives. They did not repent
They did not stop worshipping demons and fiends
Made of gold silver bronze stone wood by all possible means
Idols that cannot hear or walk or see
Blinded by their hypocrisy
They didn't turn away from their murders, their sorcery
Spells and drugs, stealing, or their sexual immorality
Another mighty angel down from heaven clothed in a cloud

Face like sun feet like fiery pillars rainbow his head endowed
He held an open written fatal plotted scroll in his hand
He put his right foot on the sea and his left foot on the land
He called out a loud voice like a lion caged and shuttered
And when he had cried seven thunders their voices uttered
When 7 thunders spoke I was about to write every last jot
Came heaven's voice Seal up 7 thunders said write them not
Then the angel I saw standing on the sea and on the land
Raised from earth toward sweet high heaven his right hand
Swore by He who lives forever Whose Spirit is ever stronger
Who created heaven, earth, sea, said 'The time is no longer.'
In the days when the seventh angel his trumpet blows
In God's mysterious purpose He will reveal what He knows
Fulfilling good news to servants, prophets as He has aired
Then a voice from heaven spoke to me, it once more declared
'Go, take the opened scroll from the angel's hand
Who is now standing on the sea and on the land.'
And I so at this written scroll I wanted to look
I went unto the angel, and said, give me the little book
He said take, it shall make thy belly bitter but eat
For in thy wide open mouth it shall be honey sweet
It was sweet as honey when I swallowed too late did I learn
It turned bitter and sour and had made my stomach churn
I was told 'Thou must prophesy again about many things.
Before many peoples, and nations, and tongues, and kings.'
And there was given me a reed like unto a rod
The angel stood saying, Rise, and measure the temple of God
Don't measure the court outside the temple, leave that out
Given to the nations for 42 months they'll trample and flout
I'll give power to my two witnesses to prophesy and go forth
For one thousand two hundred sixty days wearing sackcloth
These are 2 olive trees and candlesticks, how commanding
That before the God of earth they are now standing
If anyone wants to hurt them fire comes out
Of their mouth and burns up their enemies with a shout

So if anyone wants to hurt them mark what I say
They all have to be killed in this way
They have the power to close up the sky
So that no rain will fall for as long as they prophesy
They also have the power to turn the waters into blood
And to smite the earth with all the plagues, a wild flood
When with their testimony they are finished and done
The beast from abyss shall kill them, they shall be overrun
On streets of the great city Sodom lie bodies that have died
And Egypt, where also their Lord was crucified
And for three and a half days
Kindred peoples of nations at their dead bodies they'll gaze
And despite their sadness and their gloom
They won't let their dead bodies be put in a tomb
Those who live on earth over them will we rejoice
They will celebrate and give each other gifts a rich choice
Because these two prophets had seen that such pain was felt
Who on the face of this soil, this land, this earth had dwelt
After 3 1/2 days God's Life's breath entered them very same
Stood on their feet. Those who saw them a great fear came
Then they heard a heavenly voice, it was loud and splendid
Say to them, Come up here. And up to heaven they ascended
And as they went up to heaven riding in a bright shiny cloud
While their enemies watch them as they crush and crowd
That hour there was an earthquake, and 1/10th of the city fell
7000 people were killed by the earthquake, a doleful knell
And the rest of all this they were afraid
And so to God's glory in heaven they made
The 7th angel sounded there were voices of great accord
Saying Kingdom of this world is now kingdom of our Lord
And of his Christ he shall reign forever, and ever, all days
And he will rule forever and ever and ever and always
Then the 24 elders each on a throne
Fell on their faces to worship God alone
Giving thanks Lord God Almighty for love that is unchained

Cause you have taken your great power and have reigned
Then God's temple in heaven was unsealed
Seen in his temple the ark of his testament did yield
There were lightning, voices, dreadful, deep rattling thunder
An earthquake, and large hail putting all in fear of asunder
And in heaven a great wonderous sign was spun
There a appeared a woman clothed with the sun
Under her feet was the gracious bright moon
A crown of 12 stars on her head did festoon
And she being with child, pregnant, cried out, wailing
She was in labor, in pain from giving birth, travailing
And there appeared another wonder in heaven
And behold a great red dragon having a head of seven
And ten horns each horn redder than reds
And seven crowns upon his heads
His tail drew a 1/3rd of heaven's stars down to the earth
He stood in front of the woman who was about to give birth
So that when she gave birth upon that very hour
He, that fiery red dragon, her child he might devour
She birthed a son who is to rule all nations with an iron rod
Her child was snatched up unto the sovereign throne of God
She fled to the desert, God made a place, could go her ways
Where there she will be taken special care of for 1,260 days
War in heaven! Michael's angels the dragon they attack
Then the fiery dragon and his angels, they all fight back
But however hard and cunning they were, they prevailed not
There was no longer any place for them in heaven, not a spot
Then I heard a loud voice in heaven say
Accuser of brothers, sisters who accuses them night and day
The salvation and power and God's kingdom and its' crown
Authority of Christ before our God has been thrown down
They won cause of the Lamb's blood their witness and why?
Cause love for their own lives didn't make them afraid to die
Therefore rejoice you who in heavens dwell
But oh! The horror for the earth and sea! So much to tell

The devil has come down to you with great rage
He knows he only has a short time, a time only God can gage
The woman is given eagle's wings to fly to her desert place
Where she is fed times, and ½ a time from the serpent's face
From the snake's mouth came rivers of water in a vast spray
After the woman, that he might cause her to be carried away
But the earth helped the woman and opened its mouth
And swallowed the rivers that the dragon poured out
And the dragon with this woman had great wrath
Now he would make war on her children that was his path
On those who keep God's commandments passing wrath fell
And on those who have Jesus Christ who dare to share to tell
I stood upon the sand and saw a beast come up out of the sea
10 horns 7 crown heads on its heads the name of blasphemy
The beast I saw was like a leopard and he had bear's feet
A lion's mouth. The dragon gave it power his throne, his seat
And I saw one of his heads as it were wounded to death
Its deadly wound was healed it was breathing new breath
So the whole world wondered at this amazing feature
And what they did was to follow after this creature
They revered the dragon which gave power unto the beast
They revered the beast Who is like the beast? At very least
He was the greatest, monstrous, wild, beast they ever saw
And against whom they would never be able to go to war
The beast was given a mouth speaking blasphemies great
It was given authority to act for forty-two months straight
It opened its mouth it blasphemed against God it did yell
Blasphemed God's name, his place, (those in heaven dwell)
Also allowed to make war on saints over them victory to gain
Over all peoples and nations it was given power to attain
All on earth revered it, whose names you'll look for in vain
From when the earth was made in scroll of life of Lamb slain
If any man have an ear
He must listen, let him hear
If any are to be taken captive, then into captivity they will go

Kill with the sword, be killed with the sword, this we know
We know all of this does not come without sharp constraints
It calls for endurance, faithfulness on the part of the saints
I saw another beast from the earth it arose
Having 2 horns like lamb but it spoke dragon prose
Of the 1st beast in its presence it exercises all its might
This was quite amazing this was quite a sight
It makes the earth those who worship the 1st beast adhere
The 1st beast whose wound was healed, though so very severe
It does great signs so that even makes fire's great light
Come down from heaven to earth in people's sight
It deceives those who live on earth by the codes
Allowed to do in beast's presence and his many hot inroads
Told those on earth make beast's image heard the beast roar
Who'd been wounded by sword yet came to life once more
To the beast's image it was allowed to give breath
The image spoke anyone who didn't worship it put to death
It forces all, great, small, slaves, free, poor, rich, underfed
To have a mark put on their right hand or on their forehead
That no man may buy or sell or do any of the same
Save he had beast's mark or name or number of his name
Here is wisdom. Number of beast you should know and fix
For it is a human being's number. Its' number is 666
There was the Lamb and others, standing on Zion's Mount
His name, his father's on their foreheads 144,000, the count
Voice from heaven, the voice of many waters, thunder sharp
And I heard the voice of harpers harping with their harp
With women by them they were not defiled
These who follow the Lamb are virgins, without child
From among humankind as they were redeemed
Being the first fruits unto God and to the Lamb they beamed
No lie came from their mouths; they are without blame
Another angel flew high with eternal good news to proclaim
To them on earth, every nation, tongue, kindred and kind
Every tribe, every language, every people, assigned

'Fear God, give him glory, the hour of judgment He brings.
Worship the one who made heaven, earth, sea water springs'
A 2nd angel, 'Great Babylon is fallen, it lay in the dust.'
She made the nations drink the wine of her passion her lust
They themselves will too drink the wine of God's angry path
Poured full strength into the very cup of his blaze of wrath
With fire and brimstone he shall be tormented slowly
In the presence of the Lamb and of the angels holy
And the smoke of their torment goes up for ever and ever
No rest, for those who worship the beast or it's mark, never
This calls for endurance of the saints as each saint sees us
Who keep God's commandments and keep faith with Jesus
And I heard a voice from heaven say
Write, favored are dead who die in the Lord from this day
Yes says the Spirit it is rest from their labor they can find
Because their deeds follow them from behind
There was a white cloud there sat someone like Son of man
A gold crown on his head and a sharp sickle in his hand
Another angel came out of the temple calling in a voice loud
Use your sickle reap earth's ripe harvest to him on the cloud
So the one seated on the cloud gave his sickle one sweep
And all the earth he did reap
Another angel out of heaven's temple he didn't have a harp
No, this angel also coming out of heaven had a sickle sharp
Another angel with power over fire came out from the altar
Saying use sharp sickle cut ripe grapes on earth don't falter
Angel thrust his sickle in the earth, gathered the earth's vine
And cast it in the great winepress of the wrath of God divine
The winepress was trampled outside the city, piles and piles
Blood out of winepress high as horses' bridles for 200 miles
There were 7 angels with 7 plagues-these are the last
For with them God's anger is brought to an end, is past
And I saw as it were a sea of glass mingled with fire sharp
Those who beat the beast its image stood holding God's harp
They sing the song of Moses, God's servant, the Lamb's song

Great, and awe-inspiring, just and true, Lord God, so strong
Who won't fear you? All that come before you have kneeled
For thou are holy and your acts of justice have been revealed
After that I looked, and, behold, the temple of the tabernacle
Of the testimony in heaven it would open and unshackle
The 7 angels with the 7 plagues out the temple they came
Clothed in white linen girded with golden girdles aflame
Then one of the 4 creatures gave the 7 angels 7 gold jars
Full of the anger of God who lives longer than the stars
The temple is filled with smoke from God's glory and might
No temple entry til all 7 plagues of the 7 angels were in flight
Out of the Temple to the seven angels came a voice roaring
The seven bowls of God's anger on earth is down pouring
So the first angel poured his bowl, upon the earth it flowed
Terrible sore on beast marked people, image prayers showed
The 2nd angel poured his bowl into the sea turned blood red
Like blood of a corpse, every living thing in the sea is dead
The third angel poured out his bowl with the same aim
Upon the rivers and springs of waters, blood they became
Then I heard the angel of the waters rightly say
Thou art, was, shall be just, O Lord, in this righteous way
From shedding blood of saints, prophets, they didn't shrink
Now they're worthy of the blood you've given them to drink
And from the altar these are the words that came, too
Yes, Lord God, Almighty, your judgments are just and true
4th angel poured his bowl on the sun could he fly any higher
And power was given unto him to scorch men with fire
And the 5th angel pours out his vial upon the beast's seat
And darkness covering its kingdom is what it will meet
And by all this there upon all is such a mortal drain
That people bit their tongues because of their pain
Cursed the God of heaven for by their painful sores overrun
But they do not repent from the evils that they had done
6th angel pours his bowl on Euphrates all its greatness brings
Its water dried up so the way was ready for eastern kings

And I saw three unclean spirits like frogs come out
Of the dragon's open, bloody, foaming, mouth
The beast's mouth, a beast most abominable, too
And the mouth of the prophet most untrue
These are demonic spirits that've done, shown many a sign
Go to worldly kings battle gathered great day of God Divine
I'm coming like a thief! Look deep!
Blessed is he that watches and his garments keep
Lest he walk naked and naked he be
And his shame they see
The spirits gathered them at the place that they knew
It is called Armageddon in the tongue of the Hebrew
And the 7th angel poured out his vial into the air it was spun
Loud voice came from the temple throne saying, 'It is done!'
There were lightning strikes, voices, and thunder did roar
And a great earthquake occurred like no quake ever before
Great city split into 3 parts, cities of the nations fell into fire
God recalled great Babylon gave her winecup of furious ire
Every island fled away, was banished
And the mountains disappeared, vanished
Great heaven hail each stone weight of a talent would pound
Let loose falling upon the people found on the ground
And men blasphemed God due to this plague of the hail
Because the plague was so terrible, and so great in its scale
One of the 7 angels who had the 7 bowls spoke with me
Judgment of great whore sits on many waters I'll show thee
With her fornication was committed with the earth's kings
Those on earth are drunk on wine of her whoring, low things
Then to a desert in a Spirit-inspired trance he brought me
I saw a woman on a red beast full of names of blasphemy
7 heads, 10 horns, in purple, scarlet the woman was arrayed
She glittered with gold, jewels, pearls and pampered jade
In her hand she held a gold cup full of the vile and impure
It came from her fornication from those that she'd adjure
A name-mystery-on her forehead, a written fixation

'Babylon the great harlot mother, earth's abomination'
The woman was drunk on the blood of Jesus' martyrs
I saw that this was only the beginning only just starters
I saw she was drunk also on the blood of the saints praised
I could only wonder I was completely stunned I was amazed
The angel said to me does this amaze you?
Well now I will give an even greater clue
The woman her, 7 headed 10 horned beast, the enigma is this
Beast you saw, was, is not, is to destruction, out of the abyss
Those on earth, names haven't been written on life's scrolls
From foundation of the world, from the time the earth arose
Will be amazed when they see the beast they behold
Because the beast was, and is not, and yet is foretold
This calls for an understanding mind, wisdom and good wit
7 heads are 7 mountains on which the woman does sit
They're 7 kings 5 kings fell, 1 is, other hasn't come to place
When that king comes he must continue for a short space
As for the beast that was and is not
Itself an 8th king belongs to the 7 going to destruction to rot
10 horns you saw 10 kings who haven't received royal power
They'll receive, with the beast, royal authority for an hour
On the Lamb these shall make war
But the Lamb will emerge victorious evermore
For he is King of kings, Lord of lords
Those with him are called chosen, his faithful hordes
Then he said to me, The waters that you saw
Are peoples, crowds, nations, tongues, where sits the whore
10 horns you saw upon the beast, the whore they hate
Naked, they'll eat her flesh, burn her, and make her desolate
Because God moved them his purposes to carry out
Their realm to beast til God's words will be brought about
The woman who you saw is the great city, hers to command
That rules over all the kings of all the land
He cried mightily Babylon the great is fallen, is fallen, fallen
A home for demons, lair for every unclean spirit, she's all in

She is a lair for every unclean bird, she keeps in prison cells
Every unclean disgusting, savage, brutish, beast that repels
For it is every impudent nation
Drinks the wine of the wrath of her fornication
And the kings of the earth committed with her sexual acts
From power of her extravagance the merchants' wealth wax
Another heavenly voice, Come out of her, my people, leave
Don't take part in her sins so her plagues you don't receive
Her sins are heaven high God remembers she caused trouble
Give her what she has given to others. Give it back double
Give her back twice as much for what she has done and such
In the cup that she has poured, pour her out twice as much
To the extent that herself she glorified
Lived deliciously, extravagantly, and was full of pride
So much torment and sorrow give her, let it be
Her heart says, I'm a queen! no widow. Grief I'll never see
This is why her plagues will all come in a single day
Deadly disease, grief, and hunger will all come to prey
And she shall be with a roaring fire utterly burned
The Lord's mind is strong, with his mind on her he's turned
The earth's kings who fornicated and shared her wild ways
Shall bewail her when they see smoke of her burning ablaze
Standing afar off for the fear of her torment, how they cower
Saying Alas great Babylon thy judgment is come in one hour
Earth's merchants shall mourn over her and be heartsore
For no man buys their cargoes or merchandise anymore
Cargoes of gold, silver, jewels, pearls, silk, scarlet, linen fine
All things made of scented wood, ivory, bronze, marble, iron
Cinnamon, incense, frankincense, fragrant ointments refined
Wine oil flour wheat cattle sheep horses slaves even mankind
The fruit your whole being craved has gone from you
All things which were dainty and goodly are departed, too
You shall search behind every door, batter down every wall
And thou shalt find them no more at all
Merchants who got wealthy by her by fear will stand away

Weeping, and wailing, and mourning, they will say
The horror, great city, wore fine linen, gold that was fierce
Purple and scarlet and pearls and jewels that were scarce
In just one hour such great wealth was destroyed, razed
Sea captains sailors, traders by sea stood a way off, dazed
Seeing smoke from her burning they cried out in great pity
'What city was ever like the great city?'
On their heads they cast dust
Cried weep and wailing as they must
Alas in just one hour destroyed is the great city
Where all with ships at sea became so rich by her prosperity
Rejoice over her, heaven, you holy apostles, prophets true
Because God has condemned her as she condemned you
And a mighty angel took up a stone like a great millstone
And saying thus into the sea it was thrown
With such violence the great city Babylon will have its fall
And it will not be found anymore at all
Harpists pipers you'll never again hear their sound outpour
Trumpeters, musicians will be heard among you nevermore
And no craftsman shall be in you, whatever craft he be
The sound of a millstone shall be heard no more at all in thee
The light of a lamp will never shine again among you
Bride and groom will never be heard again among you too
Because your merchants ran the world, they ran it so fast
Because all the nations were deceived by the spell you cast
In her find blood of prophets of saints causing all such pain
Found among you all that on earth who were dead and slain
He judged the great whore, his judgments are just and true
Which did corrupt the earth with her fornication, too
The penalty for the blood of his servants he exacted
And out of her hand it was extracted
The twenty-four elders and four beasts, down they fell
Praising God on his throne, Amen Alleluia crying with a yell
And a voice came out of the throne, you could hear it call
Praise God ye servants, that fear him, both great and small

And I heard something that sounded like a huge crowd
Like rushing water and powerful thunder loud
They said Alleluia: for the Lord God omnipotent remains
Exercised his royal power! He reigns!
Be glad, rejoice, give God the honor with greatest fanfare
Marriage of Lamb is come his bride make herself prepare
And to her was given linen to wear, fine, pure and white
For fine linen is the saints' acts of justice pure and right
Then the angel said to me Write this, so that you may exam
Blessed are they called to the marriage supper of the Lamb
He said words that will stay through all times that are hard
"These are the true words of God."
Then I fell at his feet to worship him I stayed at that spot
And he said unto me, Don't! See thou do it not
I'm a servant with your brethren, just like you, just like me
Who hold firmly to Jesus' testimony it is only He that we see
Worship God! Worship God! Came these words at me
Worship God! Jesus' witness is the spirit of prophecy!
Then I saw heaven opened, and there was a horse white
Rider called Faithful and True, he judges makes war right
His eyes were full of fire, the flames were full of wrest
And on his head many royal crowns, each one a worthy crest
He had a name written on him that no man knew
Only he himself knew what was written was true
He wore a robe dyed with blood, all seek to dip
His name was called the Word of God praise from every lip
The armies which were in heaven like a military machine
Followed upon white horses clothed in fine linen white clean
From his mouth comes a sword so sharp that it will bite
He'll use it to strike the nations, against nations he'll smite
He is the one who will rule them with an iron rod
He treads the winepress of the fierce wrath of Almighty God
He has a name written on his robe and on his thigh
King of kings and Lord of lords on high
Saw an angel stand in the sun call with a loud voice and said

To all fowls that fly in the midst of heaven, high overhead
Come and gather yourselves together, meet
Unto the supper of the great God, eat
Come and eat the flesh of kings
The flesh of generals the flesh of the powerful all these things
And the flesh of horses and their riders, too
Come, eat flesh of all free, slave, both small, great, for you
The beast and the earth's kings had gathered to make war
Against him who sat on the horse his army this is what I saw
But the beast along with the false prophet was taken away
Who had done signs in the beast's presence for many a day
He had used the signs the people he was deceiving
Into worshipping the beast's mark they were receiving
The two of them then alive were thrown
Into that lake of fire burning with sulfur and brimstone
With the sword from the rider's mouth the rest he did kill
And of their flesh all the birds ate their fill
And I saw an angel come down from heaven holding in hand
The key to the bottomless pit and a great chain in a strand
He seized the dragon, the old snake, full of 1000 fears
Which is the Devil, and Satan, and bound him 1000 years
Threw him in the pit, locked and sealed over him and spun
That he deceive nations no more till the 1000 years are done
And yet, despite all this protractive, punishment and trial
After this he must be released for a little while
Then I saw thrones, and people sat one on each throne chair
And judgment was given unto them in their favor fair
They're the ones beheaded for what they'd seen and heard
The ones who had born witness to Jesus and to God's word
And those who hadn't worshipped the beast or its brand
Who hadn't received the mark on their forehead or hand
With Christ for 1000 years they lived and reigned
By His glory and grace they all had gained
Rest of dead lived not again till 1000 years were over and all
This is the first resurrection. It is what the Lord bid thee call

Blessed holy are they who in the 1st resurrection have a share
The second death has no power over them how well they fare
They will be priests of God, of Christ, and all that may entail
For 1000 years shall reign, rule, and with him shall prevail
When the 1000 years have been added up and put to use
Out of prison Satan shall be released, let out, and let loose
He'll deceive the nations doing the devil's darkest chore
Gog-and Magog, that are at the earth's corners four
To gather them to battle in bruising arms that'll haunt thee
The number of whom is as the sands of the sea
They circled the saint's camp on whom love God showered
Fire came down from God out of heaven they were devoured
Lake of fire, sulfur where beast, false prophet were forever
Where the devil is to be cast, no tear shed for him no never
For it was the devil who by them had been deceived
Thrown into that lake tormented day, night, pain unrelieved
And I saw a great white throne, and him that on it sat
Before his face earth, heaven fled no place for them on that
I saw dead, the great, the small, standing before the throne
The scrolls opened. The scroll of life, this they were shown
Things written in the scrolls about what they had done
Judged out of those things there was nowhere to run
Then the waters gave up all the dead that were in the sea
Death, Hell, delivered up the dead which were in them free
People were judged by their own damnation
Then Death, Hell were thrown in the lake of conflagration
This is the fiery lake the 2nd death a thirst impossible to slake
Anyone not written in the scroll of life thrown into fiery lake
There was a new heaven and earth, that's what I saw
And even the great sea was no more
Down from God out of heaven, new Jerusalem, the holy city
Like a bride ready for her husband, bride dressed so pretty
I heard a loud voice from the throne say,
Look! God's is dwelling here with humankind today
With men, that is what the tabernacle of God is

And the people, they all shall be his
And God shall wipe away all tears from their eyes
Neither sorrow, nor crying, no pain, and no one dies
For these former things have passed away
And it will be a brand new day
Then the one seated on the throne
Said 'Behold' and this became known
Write: for these words are faithful and true
He said, Look! I'm making all things new
Then he said to me, All is done, my friend
I am Alpha and Omega, the beginning and the end
I will give unto him that is athirst
The fountain of the water of life freely and first
They that overcome shall inherit all things they're the ones
I will be their God, and they will be my daughters and sons
But for the cowardly, the faithless, the vile, the killers
Those who commit sexual immorality, the blood spillers
Those who use drugs, sorcerers, and idolaters, and every liar
Their share will be the lake that burns with sulfur and fire
Every breath they'll pray in vain to be their last breath
For this is the second death
Then one of seven angels spoke he came from the stars
He had the seven last plagues the were filled in jars
I watched as only a heavenly angel can stride
Come he said I will show you the Lamb's wife, the bride
He carried me away in the spirit to a great mountain on high
Showed Holy Jerusalem coming out of God's heavenly sky
The city where only truth and glory of God would appear
Its brilliance like a priceless jewel like jasper crystal clear
It had a 12 gated wall with 12 angels each with nimble wing
On gates written names of the 12 tribes of Israel's offspring
3 gates on the east, three gates on the north, and the rest?
There were 3 gates on the south and 3 gates on the west
And the city had foundations, there were 12 of them, too
In them the names of the 12 apostles of the Lamb, all true

The angel who spoke to me his words came from God
And he that talked with me had a gold measuring rod
It was a golden reed with which the city to measure
The gates thereof, and the wall thereof, with pleasure
Now the city was laid out as a foursquare
Its length being the same as its width, it did share
He measured the city, it was 1500 miles, to that it came
Its breadth and width and height were all the same
He also measured the thickness of its wall
216 feet as a person or an angel might measure things at all
The wall was built of jasper. So much is unseen and untold
The city was like unto glass. It was pure gold
The 1st foundation was jasper, the 2nd was sapphire
The 3rd was chalcedony, the 4th emerald, all were half afire
The 5th sardonyx the 6th sardius the 7th chrysolite, 8th beryl
9th topaz 10th chrysoprase 11th jacinth 12th amethyst, no peril
12 gates were 12 pearls each gate was made from one pearl
And as you opened each gate through it you'd go and whirl
The city's main street was pure gold, as transparent as glass
This is God's city of gemstones and gold, as along you pass
I didn't see a temple in the city, of that there was no sign
For the Lord God Almighty and the Lamb are the shrine
The city doesn't need the moon or the sun to make it bright
Because its lamp is the Lamb, and God's glory is its light
The nations will walk by this light
Earth's kings bring glory to it, those saved and made right
Its gates will never be shut by day, there'll be no night there
They'll bring the glory and honor of the nations right there
Whatever enters it shall in no wise be unclean
Nor anyone who does what is vile and deceitful, or mean
But only those whose names are known to fit in
The Lamb's Book of Life in which they are written
And he showed me a river of water of life, pure and sheer
Flowing from the throne of God and the Lamb, crystal clear
Through the middle of the city's main street

On each side of the river is the tree of life, tis meet
Giving fruit each month tree's leaves are for healing nations
Praise God and the way of all of his creations!
And in it there shall be no curse, no curse, any more
God's Throne, Lamb, his servants will worship and adore
And they shall stand before him and see his face
And then his name on their foreheads shall be in place
Night will be no more, it is what our Lord has done
They won't need the light of a lamp or the light of the sun
For the Lord God will shine on them, light on them will pour
And they shall reign always and forevermore
Then he said to me, These words are trustworthy and true
Lord God of the holy prophets, greatest God you ever knew
Lord God of Holy prophets his angel sent
To show his servants what must soon take place, each event
Behold, I come sudden and quick
Favored he who keeps prophecy in this scroll, the one I pick
I John saw these things, and heard them, and I to see
Fell down worship at the feet angel who showed them to me
Then said he unto me, See thou do it not
For I am thy fellow servant, and of thy brethren begot
With the prophets, them who keep the sayings of this book
Worship God! He you must follow. To him you must look
Then he said unto me
Don't seal up the words of the prophecy
Contained in this scroll, let it be read over all the land
Because the time is near, yes for the time is at hand
Let those who do wrong keep doing what is wrong
Let those who are unjust let them be unjust all the day long
Let the filthy be filthy let them live in darkness and in spite
Let those who are righteous keep doing what is right
And to those who wait upon the Lord's will
Let those who are holy be holy still
And, behold, I come quickly; and my reward is with me
To give every man according as his work shall be

I am Alpha and Omega, the future, the present, the past
The beginning and the end, the first and the last
Favored are those who wash their robes they have life's tree
And they may enter in through the gates into the city
I, Jesus have sent my angel to all of you for witness to bear
About these things for the churches for you to hear
I'm the root and descendant of David, back that far
The bright morning star
For I testify unto every man
Listen as closely as you can
He who hears words of the prophecy contained in this book
If he adds to them, every plague written in this scroll he took
If anyone takes away from words of this scroll of prophecy
God will take that person's share in life's tree and holy city
And which I have written and worked with my heart whole
And from the things which are written in this scroll
He who testifies to these things says for all the world to know
Yes, I'm coming quickly Amen. Come, Lord Jesus! Even so
The grace of our Lord Jesus Christ be with you all. Amen.

Printed in the United States
by Baker & Taylor Publisher Services